**He would marry her and they'd each get what they wanted. Besides, people married every day for far less noble causes than saving two lives.**

And when it was all over, she'd go her way. He'd go his.

Maybe fate dropped a woman in a wedding dress on the side of the road for a reason.

*To hell with everything.*

Dipping his head, he took possession of those sweet lips. She dropped his hands, but he hitched an arm around her waist and dragged her closer, their bodies meeting along every line. She squirmed for a few seconds, slumped against him and then shimmied out of his grasp.

"W-what are you doing?"

"I'm kissing my bride-to-be."

# CAROL ERICSON

# THE McCLINTOCK PROPOSAL

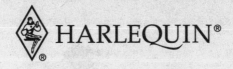

TORONTO • NEW YORK • LONDON
AMSTERDAM • PARIS • SYDNEY • HAMBURG
STOCKHOLM • ATHENS • TOKYO • MILAN • MADRID
PRAGUE • WARSAW • BUDAPEST • AUCKLAND

To the girls of SHS.
Long may we rock!

ISBN-13: 978-0-373-69498-3

THE McCLINTOCK PROPOSAL

## ABOUT THE AUTHOR

Carol Ericson lives with her husband and two sons in Southern California, home of state-of-the-art cosmetic surgery, wild freeway chases, palm trees bending in the Santa Ana winds and a million amazing stories. These stories, along with hordes of virile men and feisty women clamor for release from Carol's head. It makes for some interesting headaches until she sets them free to fulfill their destinies and her readers' fantasies. To find out more about Carol, her books and her strange headaches, please visit her Web site at www.carolericson.com, "where romance flirts with danger."

## Books by Carol Ericson

HARLEQUIN INTRIGUE
1034—THE STRANGER AND I
1079—A DOCTOR-NURSE ENCOUNTER
1117—CIRCUMSTANTIAL MEMORIES
1184—THE SHERIFF OF SILVERHILL
1231—THE McCLINTOCK PROPOSAL

Don't miss any of our special offers. Write to us at the following address for information on our newest releases.

Harlequin Reader Service
U.S.: 3010 Walden Ave., P.O. Box 1325, Buffalo, NY 14269
Canadian: P.O. Box 609, Fort Erie, Ont. L2A 5X3

# CAST OF CHARACTERS

**Callie Price**—A bride on the run from her criminal fiancé, Callie sets her sights on a temperamental cowboy to rescue her and help her get control of an inheritance from her grandfather. But her simple plan becomes complicated…and dangerous.

**Rod McClintock**—With his ranch in trouble, Rod agrees to Callie's wild scheme to marry her, but he does so more to protect the free-spirited artist than to benefit himself.

**Bobby Jingo**—This small-time crook has some big-time plans, and Callie's inheritance figures prominently in his future.

**Jonah Price**—Unfortunately, Callie's father enjoys wine, women and gambling.

**Grady Pierce**—He belongs to one of Silverhill's oldest ranching families and isn't happy when Callie comes to town to claim her inheritance, an inheritance that could've fallen into his lap.

**Amber Lewis**—New in town, Amber seems to want to make Callie her new best friend. Is it just friendship she wants?

**Dana McClintock**—Rod's sister-in-law may be related to Callie by more than marriage. Callie wants to believe in family, but all hers ever gave her was grief. Will Dana be any different?

**Jesse Price**—The boy Callie plans to adopt needs a stable home, but Callie worries that making him her son will expose him to the danger that surrounds her.

# Chapter One

The crystal beads bounced on the hardwood floor and scattered in all directions. Callie Price hung over the windowsill, her legs, tangled in silk organza, dangling toward the ground. She bicycled her legs, the toes of her white satin pumps grappling for purchase on terra firma.

She tumbled into the flowerbed, the train of her dress burying her beneath layers of white froth. Scrambling to her feet, she jumped out of the flowers, leaving one of the pumps in the moist dirt.

For a scumbag, Bobby Jingo sure liked his flowers.

She slipped off the other shoe and tossed it at its mate. She never could run in heels.

The damp grass squished beneath her feet as she backed away from the window. Then she spun around and took the corner of the house at high speed. She collided with a teenage boy, knocking the cigarette from his lips and a can of beer from his hand.

"Whoa!" He held up his empty hands, his eyes widening as his gaze swept from her veil to her bedraggled train. "Aren't you the bride?"

Callie glanced at the red vest and pert bow tie, incongruous over a pair of black jeans and motorcycle boots. Her eyes flicked to the can on the ground, spewing foam. "Aren't you one of the valet parking attendants?"

Shoving his hands in his pockets, the boy squared his shoulders. "C'mon, I had two sips, and I need to get paid for this gig tonight. I owe my friend some money."

"There's a lot of that going around."

"Huh?"

"Tell you what." Callie yanked off the veil and dropped it on top of the smoldering cigarette, then kicked it toward the beer. Starting a fire wouldn't be a great idea right now. "You get me some transportation out of here, and I won't tell anyone you've been drinking on the job."

The teen gulped, his Adam's apple prominent in his pencil-thin neck. "Are you kidding?"

She pointed to her feet encased in shimmering hose and the dirt-smudged train. "Do I look like I'm kidding?"

He shook his head, a smile spreading across his face. "Are you running out on the wedding?"

Real genius, this one, but he just might be her savior. "Yeah, I've got pressing business elsewhere."

"Sweet." He grabbed her arm and pulled her to the back of the house. Pointing to a beat-up motorcycle leaning precariously on its kickstand, he said, "Take it."

"Is—is it yours?" The boy sure seemed eager to part with his bike, or maybe he wanted in on the adventure.

He dug into his pocket and pulled out a key. As it dangled from his finger, it caught the light and winked at her. *No time to analyze his motives,* she knew.

She snatched the key from his hand, lifted up her skirt and rushed toward the bike. She called over her shoulder, "How do I get it back to you?"

He waved an arm. "Leave it on the side of the highway or something. It has a full tank—almost."

Reaching beneath her dress, she peeled off the silk pantyhose and hung them on a cactus. She shoved the key into the ignition and turned back toward the teenager, his mouth hanging open as he wrestled another cigarette out of a pack. "One more thing."

"Do you want me to show you how to start the bike up and keep it going?"

"I know how to ride a motorcycle." She tugged at the train hanging from her backside. "Could you rip this damn thing off my dress?"

FIVE MINUTES LATER, shoeless, veilless and trainless, Callie roared north on I-25 away from Las Cruces.

Once she got back to L.A. she'd figure out another way to save her father. She just hoped she could come up with something before Bobby hurt Dad.

Who was she kidding? After the stunt she just pulled, Bobby might hurt her, too.

ROD MCCLINTOCK WORRIED THE toothpick at the side of his mouth as his gaze drilled the highway, shrouded in purple dusk. The horses he looked at in Austin would be a good start for the dude ranch, but he hated incurring so much debt.

He needed an infusion of money, land or a fairy godmother. Or maybe all three.

Through a layer of dust, a shimmering white shape appeared on the side of the highway. Either his fairy godmother just appeared or he could use a drink.

Easing off the gas pedal, he swerved to the left and peered out the passenger window. An old Honda bike tilted on its kickstand, and a woman in a long white dress stood beside it, waving her arms over her head.

A couple of cars had already sped past her, and a few cars behind him slowed down to take in the spectacle. He'd let one of those drivers take care of the stranded motorist. He didn't need any more problems in his life.

He watched his rearview mirror as a black SUV pulled behind the woman and the motorcycle. Three men tumbled out of the car, clutching bottles. Rod made for the shoulder of the highway and threw his truck into Reverse.

By the time he jumped out of his truck, the three men had formed a circle around the woman, the white wedding dress swirling around her legs. Her long, blond hair whipped in the hot wind from the speeding cars on the highway.

"Hey, baby, did your groom ditch you by the side of the road or something?"

The woman tilted up her chin, digging her fists into her hips. She looked ready to make a run at the guy.

"Take a hike." Rod stepped between the man and the stranded woman, jerking his thumb toward the idling SUV.

"Are you the groom?" The moron twisted his head over his shoulder and snorted at his two buddies.

Rod grabbed a handful of the man's sweat-dampened T-shirt and yanked him forward. The man's head snapped back around, his mouth slack with a dribble of beer at the corner.

"Get moving." Rod bunched his fist and drew it back to emphasize his point.

The man pedaled backward, bumping into his two friends, already scrambling for the security of the car. "Sure, man. We're not looking for trouble."

Only with a little blonde in a wedding dress and…bare feet.

The men piled into the SUV and shot down the highway.

Holding up his index finger, Rod pulled out his cell phone and placed a call to 911, giving them the license plate of the SUV. He snapped the phone shut and dropped it back into his shirt pocket. "Don't want those guys plowing into a carload of kids."

She gathered her billowing hair in one hand and twisted it behind her. "Who are you, Sir Galahad?"

"You're welcome."

A pink blush washed over her cheeks beneath the grit and grime. "Thanks. I appreciate your help. I was so happy someone pulled over—until I saw The Three Stooges climb out of the car."

"You're in a dangerous situation." His gaze narrowed. "What *is* your situation?"

"I ran out of gas." She aimed a dirty, pink-polished toe at the tire of the Honda 550, but stopped short of kicking it.

Running out of gas didn't tell half the story of a barefoot, bedraggled bride in the middle of New Mexico. He tapped the phone in his pocket. "Do you want me to call a roadside service to bring you some gas?"

The woman laced her hands in front of her and dropped her chin, glancing up at him through lowered lashes.

A practiced look, if he ever saw one.

"Not really. I was kind of hoping for a lift. It's been a hell of a ride in this wedding gown."

"What about the bike?"

She shrugged, the strap of her dress slipping off her shoulder. "It's not mine."

Rod crossed his arms and dug his boot heels into the gravel. If she stole the motorcycle, he'd turn her in, too, with those jackasses in the car.

She peered at him through the veil of hair that hung over her face, and then jerked her head up. "I didn't steal the bike. Someone loaned it to me."

He cocked his head. This one looked like a package of trouble tied up with a white bow; but curiosity nibbled at his gut. He hoped to hell that curiosity wouldn't land him in the same condition as the cat.

"How are you going to return the bike to your... friend?"

"He told me to leave it on the side of the road when I ran out of gas, and he'd get it back." She nibbled at her bottom lip and crinkled her brow, as if the logic of this plan escaped even a barefoot woman standing in the middle of the highway in a dirty wedding dress.

His gaze tracked over the motorcycle—no saddlebags, no pouch, no nothing. "Do you have a purse with you? Money? Change of clothing?"

She threw her head back and laughed at the darkening sky. Then she doubled over, her shoulders shaking as she clutched her stomach. Was she having a breakdown?

Rod stepped toward her, his boots crunching the gravel, and her head shot up. Tears streamed down her face, and she swept them away, creating streaks of dirt on her cheeks. But she was still laughing.

"Do I look like I have anything? Just a few bucks and my driver's license." She patted the side of her breast, encased in the tight bodice of the wedding dress. "Wouldn't want to get a ticket for driving without a license."

A carload of teenagers screamed and yelled out their car window, and the woman rubbed a hand across her nose. "Can we get off of this godforsaken highway now?"

"After you." In a grand gesture, he swept his arm toward his truck. "Where are you headed?"

Taking a few tentative steps on the chunky gravel, she called over her shoulder, "North is good."

Rod resisted the urge to sweep her off her feet, which must be hurting. Better to let her tough it out than suspect him of improper designs on her. Although accepting a ride from a stranger didn't seem to bother her.

Reaching the truck, she grabbed the door handle before he could, and pulled herself onto the running board. Nudging her hand out of the way, he opened the door for her. She launched herself inside, dropping onto the leather interior of his truck with a rustle of silk and a soft sigh.

By the time he slid into the driver's seat, the woman had adjusted the seat back as far as it would go, stretched her legs out and closed her eyes.

He studied her face in the creeping gloom, the headlights of the passing cars illuminating its planes and curves. She'd obviously ditched a wedding and, judging by her dress, it was her own. But why the full-scale flight in complete bridal regalia? She couldn't stop to change clothes, grab a credit card, get her own car? The whole thing smelled worse than a truckload of manure.

She opened one eye. "Are you going to put this behemoth in gear and get moving?"

For a woman in her position, she didn't show much gratitude. He stuck out his hand. "My name's Rod."

She placed her delicately boned hand in his and, with the grip of a truck driver, she said, "Callie."

He extracted his fingers from hers and cranked on the engine, Bach immediately cascading from the speakers. She raised one perfectly sculpted eyebrow, and he jabbed the button to turn off the CD player.

Blowing out a breath, he pulled onto the highway. "So, how'd a nice girl like you wind up on the roadside in a wedding dress?"

"Who said I was nice?" She clicked open his glove compartment and rummaged inside with one hand.

"Looking for something?"

"Food. I'm starving. Didn't stick around long enough for the canapés at the reception."

Despite being an intruder, she'd made herself right at

home in his truck. "There's a bag in the backseat with some granola bars and beef jerky, and a cooler with some bottled water."

"Even that sounds good to me right now." She unsnapped her seat belt and twisted in her seat to paw through the paper bag on the floor of the truck.

Rod shot her a sidelong glance as she ripped into a piece of jerky with straight, white teeth. If he had any sense, he'd turn around and deliver her back to the bridegroom. Poor sap. What kind of woman leaves her man stranded at the altar?

She chugged the water and then rested the bottle against her cheek, staring at the highway as his truck gobbled it up. Her pretty blue eyes, shadowed by the dark interior of his car, had a haunted look. Her porcelain skin stretched too tightly over her high cheekbones, and her full lips pursed into a tight knot.

Okay, maybe she didn't dump a poor sap. Rod always jumped to the most unsavory conclusions about women and their motives—a legacy from mommy dearest.

He cleared his throat. "Are you hungry? Because I've been driving all afternoon, up from Austin, and I could use a meal."

Callie flashed him a smile, and his heart almost came to a crashing halt in his chest. The woman could crack wise with the best of them, but that smile didn't contain an ounce of artifice or bitterness.

"That would be great. And once we get to the next town, maybe you could loan me some money so I can hop on a bus, or at least loan me your cell phone to call a friend back home to wire me some money or something."

"Back home? You're not from around here?"

"L.A."

His brows shot up. "What's an L.A. girl doing in New Mexico?"

"Isn't it obvious?" She tugged at the sides of the wedding gown, ripping off a little more lace.

"Okay, let me get this straight." He loosened his grip on the steering wheel and flexed his fingers. "You came out from L.A. to New Mexico…Arizona…Texas to get married, decided you couldn't go through with it, hightailed it out of your own wedding and hopped on a motorcycle to escape. Is that about right?"

She flashed him two thumbs up. "You got it."

"So, are you heading back to L.A. now?"

"Uh-huh."

He didn't believe half of that story, but once he dropped her at the next bus stop, her story wouldn't matter anymore. Then he could get back to his own problems of raising enough money to turn his working ranch into a dude ranch.

Since his father and stepmother moved to Palm Springs, taking most of the capital out of the ranch for their retirement, he'd have to rely on loans to get his dude ranch up and running. He hated being indebted to anyone, even a bank.

The McClintock spread had enough space for a modest dude ranch, but he needed more land to really make a go of it.… Not that he could afford to buy more land. Or more horses.

He rolled his shoulders and glanced at his silent companion. It didn't look like she had any intention of satisfying his curiosity, but at least she had a plan. He didn't want her depending on him to come to the rescue.

"Truth or Consequences."

"Huh?" She swiveled her head around and held up her hands. "I'm not up for playing any games."

He chuckled and pointed to the illuminated sign looming ahead. "That's the name of the next town. Ever been there?"

"No. How'd it get a name like that?"

"Has something to do with the game show. It used to be called Hot Springs."

"What a relief. I thought the name might be a requirement for entry into the town."

Rod curved around the off ramp to Truth or Consequences, gripping the steering wheel. Callie definitely had something to hide. He didn't find it surprising that a woman had secrets. He never met a woman who didn't, but he couldn't figure out why he was so hell-bent on discovering hers.

He pulled into the parking lot of a casual restaurant on the main drag. "I'd offer you some other clothes, but all I have is a sweatshirt. Do you think you'd look more, or less conspicuous with a sweatshirt pulled over that dress?"

Callie pulled down the visor and flipped up the mirror to check her reflection, the first time she did so since climbing into his truck. Pretty women usually worried more about their appearance. Of course, she had other issues on her mind.

Wrinkling her nose, she plucked some tissues from the box in his console. She dabbed at the few smudges left on her face and ran her hands through her tangled hair.

"Sitting at a table, nobody will even notice the bridal attire. I'll take the sweatshirt."

Rod reached into the backseat and dropped his gray sweatshirt into her lap. She shook it out and read the front. "Texas A&M. Your alma mater?"

"Yep." He got out of the car and walked around to open the passenger door for her while she struggled to pull the sweatshirt over her head. "Let me help you. You're trying to put your head through the armhole."

He shifted the sweatshirt so that a crown of golden hair appeared at the neck, and then yanked it down. Running his hand under what hair was still stuffed in the sweatshirt, he swept it free. His fingers lingered in the soft strands before he jerked his hand away, as if scorched.

She blinked and tossed her blond mane over one shoulder. Did she notice his reluctance to relinquish her hair? At least she didn't have a smart-ass comment for the occasion.

He pointed to her bare feet. "I hope that won't be a problem. The dress is long enough that your lack of footwear may not be noticeable."

"I'll shuffle along behind you." She jumped down from the truck, her feet landing on the asphalt of the parking lot with a slap.

A few curious looks and a couple of smirks meandered their way as they entered the restaurant and settled into a booth by the window, but the waitress didn't seem to notice anything awry. They ordered sandwiches and fries, and iced tea for her and a beer for him. He needed that drink now.

Callie excused herself to wash her face and hands in the ladies' room. When she returned, Rod dug his elbows into the Formica table, resting his chin on his hands. "Since we're in Truth or Consequences, how about some truth? Why'd you run out on your own wedding?"

She looked up from dumping artificial sweetener in her tea. "I decided I didn't want to marry my fiancé."

"Just like that?"

"The idea had been stewing awhile." She held the empty package of sweetener close to her face, as if studying the ingredients.

"Why didn't you call it off before the actual wedding day?"

"It's complicated." She crushed the package in her hand and flicked it across the tabletop.

"And why the escape on a motorcycle? That's a little dramatic."

He shifted in his seat as her lips puckered around a straw. If this woman left him standing at the altar, he'd be consumed with anger, worry and…frustration for missing out on the wedding night.

"I guess I chickened out. I couldn't walk in there and tell everyone I decided to cancel the wedding, so I took off. One of the valet parking attendants loaned me his bike. The rest is recent history."

It still seemed like an odd way to cancel a wedding. "Will your scorned groom follow you to L.A.?"

Her eyes widened. "He knows better than that. Enough about my boring story. What about you? Where are you headed?"

If Callie thought ditching a wedding and fleeing on a motorcycle in a wedding gown constituted boredom, his life would put her to sleep.

"I'm heading back home after looking at some horses in Austin. Seeing you on the side of the road in that dress spiced up my journey."

She tilted her head. "You have a fantastic face."

His beer went down the wrong way and he choked. "What the hell does that mean?"

She extended her arms, her wiggling fingers inches from his face. "A strong, proud face. Do you mind?"

He had no idea what she planned to do, but he nodded anyway. For some crazy reason, he found it almost impossible to deny this woman anything. Good thing he intended to drop her at a bus stop soon.

Her smooth fingertips traced along his jawline, and then the pads of her fingers danced across his cheekbones. She ran her thumb down the bridge of his nose and caressed his forehead. Despite her light touch, he felt her probing his depths, reading every line on his face. He didn't want it to end, but people were beginning to stare.

He caught her wrists. "What are you doing?"

Hunching her shoulders, she grinned. "I'm a sculptor. Sometimes I get carried away when I see a great face."

An artist? That explained a lot. The few artists he knew lived scattered, self-centered lives. He dropped his hold on her and wrapped his hands around his sweating bottle, welcoming its coolness.

"Why do you need horses?"

She always managed to shift the focus back to him. "I own a ranch."

"A ranch?"

"I'm planning to turn it into a dude ranch. You know, riding lessons, roping cattle, that kind of thing? It's hard to make a profit on a midsize, working ranch these days."

The waitress set down their plates with a clatter, and Rod grabbed his sandwich and took a big bite. He'd never admitted that to anyone outside his family. Maybe Callie's reticence led him to fill the gap with his own personal revelations.

He may be in Truth or Consequences, but that didn't mean he had to play the game. He wiped tomato juice from his chin with a napkin and asked, "What do you sculpt?"

"Interesting faces."

THEY SPENT THE NEXT HALF HOUR talking about art and ranching in general terms. Callie skirted and danced around personal facts like a pro. He recognized the maneuvers as ones he used himself.

As Rod paid the bill, he asked the waitress the location of the nearest bus depot.

"If you go about two blocks up the street and make a left on Navajo, there's a bus stop on your right. You can catch a bus there to the depot in Albuquerque, if that's where you're headed."

"That would be perfect. If you could loan me the bus fare to L.A., I'll pay you back when I get home." Callie grabbed a napkin from the dispenser and a pen from the check tray. "Give me your address and I'll send you the money to pay back the loan."

"Don't worry about it. You don't have to pay me back."

She gripped the pen, her knuckles turning white. "I always pay my debts."

Rod covered her hand with his, smoothing his thumb across her silky skin. "It's not a loan. It's a gift…a wedding gift."

Her fist unclenched, as one corner of her mouth lifted in a half smile. "There was no wedding, remember?"

"How about a thank-you gift then, for breaking up a long, tedious journey."

"I guess I can accept that."

He excused himself to use the men's room, leaving her at the table doodling on the napkin. When he returned, her presence almost surprised him. She seemed as elusive as a puff of dandelion on the wind.

His visceral response of pleasure when he saw her surprised him even more. It had been a long time since he'd had more than a superficial interest in a woman.

They climbed back into the truck and crawled down Main Street, looking for Navajo. As they rounded the corner toward the bus stop, Rod said, "I can drive you to Albuquerque."

"No. You've already done more than enough—a ride, a meal, bus fare. I don't want to put you out more than I already have. I'll be fine once I get on that bus."

Rod helped her out of his truck for the last time and reached for his wallet. "If you have time in Albuquerque, and the bus depot is near a store, you should buy yourself some shoes."

Callie stood on tiptoe to read the bus schedule while he thumbed through the bills in his wallet. He had no idea how much a ticket to L.A. would cost, but it had to be more than the cash in his wallet.

"How much longer do you have to wait for the next bus to Albuquerque?"

She squinted at the sign. "About forty-five minutes."

"Good. That'll give me some time to run across the street to that ATM to get some more cash, and then maybe we can find you some shoes."

"Rod, please. You have to let me repay you. You would be home with your wife and kids by now if you hadn't stopped to rescue me from those idiots in the SUV." She tilted her head, studying his face.

She seemed to be making a lot of assumptions. He never told her where his ranch was located. For all she knew, it could be up in Montana. And he definitely didn't tell her about any wife and kids.

"I'm not married, and I don't have any kids that I know of, although in my family, that doesn't mean much."

She drew her brows together, and he laughed. "Long story about my brothers. Stay here while I get some money."

He waited for a few cars to pass before jogging across the street. He'd come a long way from when he first passed

Callie on the highway, but he never could leave a damsel in distress—which usually led to problems. Whenever he rescued a woman, she usually expected something more from him, and he never wanted to deliver on that something more.

He felt differently about Callie, probably because in another forty-five minutes she'd be out of his life forever. No expectations there.

The ATM sucked in the card and he punched in his code. Just as the machine began spitting twenties at him, he heard a squeal of tires.

He glanced over his shoulder at a white Cadillac with spinning rims pulling up to the bus stop. His mouth dropped open as Callie lifted her skirts and took off in the opposite direction of the car.

Grabbing his card and cash, Rod spun around and sprinted across the street. A man burst out of the Caddy as it lurched into a U-turn. The stranger lunged for Callie, her long dress encumbering her escape.

The man grabbed a handful of Callie's dress and yanked her backward. She tottered for a moment, like the bride on top of a wedding cake sinking into the frosting, before tumbling sideways. As she fell, she screamed, "I'm not going back."

Rod's heart thundered in his chest. Callie's bridegroom had tracked her down.

And he wanted a bride.

## Chapter Two

Callie's attacker landed on top of her as they both crashed to the ground. The fall sucked the air out of her lungs and she gasped for breath. Inhaling grit from the sidewalk, she bucked and squirmed beneath the man to throw him off. She twisted onto her back and swiped at the man's face, drawing blood.

She recognized him as one of Bobby's associates, Clyde.

He cursed and rose to his knees, straddling her body. "You're going back to Bobby, and I'm going to deliver you."

Like some terrible, avenging superhero, Rod appeared, looming behind Clyde. Rod hitched an arm around Clyde's neck and yanked him back. His weight shifted to Callie's thighs and she reached over her head to grab a pole, trying to pull her legs free.

Clyde's face above Rod's corded forearm reddened as he choked and sputtered. After a minute of clawing at Rod's unyielding arm, Clyde slumped to the side, slack-jawed.

Callie slid her legs from beneath his inert body. As she staggered to her feet, the driver of the Cadillac hooked an arm around her waist. He dragged her toward the open door of the car, lifting her off her feet. She drummed her heels against his shins and dug her fingernails into his arm.

Rod delivered a final blow to the prostrate lump on the ground and then charged the man holding Callie. He slammed his fist into the man's face, which spurted blood.

"Damn you, stay out of this." Her abductor released her and barreled into Rod, who welcomed his advance with a kick to the midsection.

As the driver doubled over, Rod grabbed Callie's hand and they sprinted to his truck. Ever the gentleman, even in a time of crisis, Rod opened her door and lifted her onto the seat. He slid into the driver's seat and turned the ignition.

He pulled away from the curb, and a sharp crack propelled Callie about two feet off the seat. "What the hell was that?"

"Your scorned groom took a shot at us."

"That's not my groom. He sent his cohorts to do his dirty work." Clutching her belly, she peered into the side mirror. "Are they following us?"

"Not yet, but let's make it hard for them." Rod skidded around the corner, and then another, before careening down an alleyway. He dug his cell phone out of his pocket.

"Who are you calling?"

"The police."

She grabbed his arm. "You can't do that."

"Why not? Two men tried to kidnap you. Even ditching a wedding doesn't justify that."

"It's not that simple, Rod." She covered her face with her hands, massaging her temples with her fingertips. He had to know she'd given him only the barest of details. The way he'd studied her with his guarded green eyes told her that much. He didn't trust her as far as he could throw her. Peeking at his bulging bicep through her fingers, she decided she'd chosen the wrong analogy.

Rod slammed on the brakes, and she lurched forward, straining against her seat belt.

"What are you doing?" She glanced at his profile, as rock-hard as his bicep, as he clenched the steering wheel with hands still bloody from the fight.

"You tell me what's not so simple, Callie. I want to know everything. Right now."

Licking her lips, she craned her neck around to look out the back window. "I'll explain everything, but can we get out of Truth or Consequences first?"

He peeled away from the curb and headed for the on-ramp for I-25...south. She swallowed. "Y-you're not taking me back, are you?"

He snorted. "Why would I want to deliver you into the hands of your irate groom and deprive myself the pleasure of strangling you myself?"

He jabbed a button on the console and classical music filled the truck as he dragged in a deep breath.

"You're kidding...aren't you?"

He snorted again, but he'd loosened his grip on the steering wheel and the harsh lines at the sides of his mouth disappeared.

The desert landscape whizzed by, and the cacti hunched like little alien creatures with their arms raised to the sky, begging to return home. She could relate—not that L.A. held any charm for her anymore, except for her foster child Jesse, but she wanted to get back to her makeshift studio. She had the perfect subject for her next sculpture. Her gaze slid to the silent man beside her, his thumbs tapping in time to the music from the CD.

Could she tell Rod everything? When she had his face

beneath her hands, she knew he'd accept nothing less than the truth. When he'd rescued her from those three morons on the side of the road, she knew a woman could depend on him. And yet… The man had his own demons to slay. Years of photographing and sculpting faces had taught her a thing or two about reading people.

*Yeah, like you did such a good job reading Bobby Jingo.*

She'd been watching the highway since they left Truth or Consequences. When a pair of headlights came up behind, Rod would slow down until the car passed them. No white Cadillac so far. Had Bobby's men continued north? She shivered and clutched her bare arms.

"Are you cold?" Rod turned down the music and flipped off the air conditioning.

"No." If Bobby had tracked her down, what had he done to her father? She gripped her hands in her lap. She'd better find out. "Can I borrow your cell phone to call my father?"

"If your father was at the wedding, do you think that's a good idea?"

"Even if Bobby's monitoring Dad's calls, what's he going to do with your cell phone number?"

"Harass me."

She held out her hand. "You're a big boy. You just single-handedly disposed of two of Bobby's goons. What's a little harassment?"

Rod plucked his phone out of his shirt pocket and dropped it into her open palm. "Be careful. Don't tell him anything."

Nodding, she punched in her father's cell phone number. Dad picked up after the first ring.

"Dad, it's me."

He coughed. "What are you up to, Slim?"

He'd never called her Slim before. Didn't much bother with nicknames. "Is Bobby there?"

"Yep. I bet on that pony once. Why'd you bet on him? Why'd you do it?"

"I'm sorry, Dad. I—I overheard a conversation." She sent a sidelong glance toward Rod. "After that, I couldn't go through with it."

"That pony put me in a tight spot."

She clenched her jaw. "Are you okay? Has he hurt you?"

"Not yet. And I'll make sure he doesn't. What are you going to do now?"

"I'm not sure, but I'll get you out of this. I promise."

Her father grunted, and then Bobby's rough voice assaulted her over the line. "Where are you, bitch? I guess you found out that dear old Dad didn't screw me over in a business deal. What else did you discover? My men told me you're with some cowboy who rushed you off in his truck."

"Did they also tell you that cowboy kicked their asses before we rushed off in his truck?"

Rod jerked his head around. "Is that him?"

Bobby cursed. "Nobody can protect you and nobody can protect your father. He owes me over a hundred grand for a gambling debt, and he's going to pay. Then you're going to—"

Rod snatched the phone from her hand. "Listen, you sonofabitch, the next time you send a couple of jokers after Callie, I'll send them back to you with more than a few cuts and bruises. I'll send them back to you in matching body bags."

He snapped the phone shut and tossed it into the cup holder. Callie laughed. She grabbed the phone, powered down her window, and tossed it out.

Rod jerked his head around. "Why'd you do that?"

"Bobby might be able to trace your phone and track us down." She brushed her hands together as if ridding herself of a pesky bug.

In the few months she'd known Bobby Jingo, she never heard anyone talk to him like that before. It gave her confidence that she could handle the man. Rod gave her confidence.

"Is your father okay?"

"For now. Where are we going?"

"Here." He took the next exit toward Hillsboro. "Hillsboro is a ghost town, an old mining town."

"You're taking me to a ghost town?" Gooseflesh rose on her arms. She didn't need any more scares tonight.

"Only one part of it is ghostly. People still live in Hillsboro. There are even a few art galleries."

Leaning over, she peered at the digital clock on the dashboard. "I'll bet you there's nobody awake in Hillsboro at eight-thirty on a Saturday night. Except the ghosts."

"We're not going there to kick up our heels."

Twenty minutes later, they tooled along Main Street. A few shops had their lights on, and Callie didn't see one ghost.

Rod pulled up next to a church. They got out of the truck, walked up to the church and stood on the bottom step. "We can see every car that comes into town from here."

"And if one of them is a white Caddy?"

"Bring it." He patted the black fanny pack he'd buckled around his hips when he got out of the truck.

She raised her brows and smirked. "You're going to beat them back with the contents of a fanny pack?"

"This is a gun bag, not a fanny pack, and the contents include one Smith&Wesson pistol."

"Oh." She gulped. Maybe he wasn't kidding about those body bags. "Where'd you get that?"

"Beneath the seat of my truck."

Good thing she didn't see that when he first picked her up, or she'd have jumped out of the truck on the interstate. Now that cold metal made her feel warm and fuzzy.

He grabbed her hand and led her to the top step. "Do you want to go inside?"

"Are guns allowed in churches?"

"Ever hear 'Praise the Lord and pass the ammunition'?"

She giggled, and it released a little knot in her chest. She could do this. She could trust Rod.

"I think I'd rather keep an eye on the road." She sank to the church step, the skirt of the wedding dress billowing around her.

Right location. Right dress. Wrong occasion.

Rod perched next to her, his thigh brushing her leg. Her eyelids fluttered at the sweet sensation.

She couldn't believe her good fortune when this hunk of cowboy strode out of his truck to rescue her. At least one bit of luck had scrabbled through the misery of her wedding day and the past six months of her life.

"Okay, start from the beginning. Come clean, so I know what I'm dealing with when I drive you into Albuquerque and see you on that train to L.A."

"Bus."

"Train. Circumstances have changed."

She crossed her legs at the ankles and tapped her feet together. How could she start from the beginning? They'd be here until mass the next morning.

It all started with her lunatic grandfather and his

draconian conditions of inheritance. But she had to start somewhere.

"I agreed to marry a loan shark, Bobby Jingo, to pay off my father's debts."

Rod twitched, his thigh banging against hers. "Are you kidding me?"

"No. But at the time, I didn't realize Bobby was a loan shark." Or a wannabe drug dealer, the worst of the worst, but she kept that deal breaker to herself. "My father told me he had promised some money to Bobby in a business deal, and thanks to my father's mismanagement, the deal fell through and Bobby lost a lot of money because of it."

"That shows an amazing degree of familial loyalty." His rough hand cupped her face, and he turned it toward him so he could look into her eyes. She blinked, but met his gaze steadily. "Why would you do something like that?"

"I wanted to help out my father and maybe help myself a little, too. A few months before my father's phone call, a fire damaged my studio in L.A. I lost all my art in that fire, and my home."

Callie bit her lip. She also lost her opportunity to adopt Jesse, a foster child she'd met while giving art lessons.

He squeezed her shoulder. "Isn't there another way you can raise the money? Get a loan from a bank? Sell a car? Take equity out of a property?"

She shook her head, drawing her knees to her chest. "Neither of us has any collateral or property...*yet.* I just couldn't think of another way to help him."

Rod grunted. "Maybe he doesn't deserve your help. What kind of father allows his daughter to marry a scumbag to save his hide?"

"A bad one." She lifted her shoulders. Even though

she'd given up on a father-knows-best type of dad, it didn't mean she could stand by and watch someone break his kneecaps—or worse. "Dad's not all bad. It was my idea. He did try to talk me out of it."

"Bull. He misrepresented the situation to you to rope you in. How much money are we talking about?"

"One hundred and thirty thousand, give or take a few grand."

Rod whistled. "That's some gambling habit. No wonder you can't sell a car to pay back the money, unless you have a Ferrari."

"Dad bets on the ponies, sports, loves Vegas. You name it, he'll take odds. I should've known his debt involved gambling and not business."

"Ah, I don't mean to be insulting." Rod cleared his throat. "But is this thug really willing to accept a reluctant bride in exchange for a hundred and thirty grand?"

"This is where it gets good." She wrapped her arms around her legs and balanced her chin on her knees.

"It hasn't been good yet?"

"Once I marry, I *will* have the money."

Rod buried his fingers in his thick, sandy-blond hair. "Now I'm confused. Why will you have money when you marry Bobby Jingo?"

"I didn't say I had to marry Bobby Jingo, just marry. My grandfather had some crazy ideas. He always wanted a big family, and he built a sprawling house on his ranch in Wyoming to accommodate it. Unfortunately, he and my grandmother had only one child, my father. Then my father turned out to be irresponsible and immature. He married several times, but he had only one child with his second wife—me. At least, I think Mom held the honored position of wife number two."

"How many times has your father been married?"

Rod's eyes looked a little glazed over, but he was obviously following the story without too much difficulty.

"Oh, I don't know." She waved her arms breezily. "Four or five times."

"So this lack of familial dedication to the old homestead gave your grandfather his crazy ideas?"

"You could say that. Before he died, he drew up a will stating that his sole grandchild, me, would inherit the ranch only when I married."

"And Bobby Jingo obviously knew about this will."

"My father told him."

"Great guy, your father."

"We've already covered that aspect of this story, but Dad didn't believe I'd actually offer myself to Bobby. When he first called me, he was kind of hoping I already had someone in mind."

"At the last minute you couldn't go through with it, even to save your father?"

"I wanted to. I really did. I figured, once I married Bobby and sold the ranch, I could go back to L.A. But then I overheard him talking to someone and discovered he wasn't the injured party in the business deal, or not exactly." A tremble snaked its way up her spine, a sob escaping her lips.

Wrapping an arm around her, Rod drew her close. Her head dropped to his solid shoulder, and he smoothed her hair from her cheek. The warmth from his body soaked through the satin of her dress, and her fears evaporated.

She didn't want the moment to end. She didn't want to tell Rod everything she overheard that convinced her she couldn't marry Bobby. She wanted to push the ugly truth into the background.

If she'd gone ahead with the marriage, she would've jeopardized her adoption of Jesse. She'd figured a marriage would improve her chances at adoption, but not a marriage to someone like Bobby Jingo.

The curve of Rod's arm represented a safety and contentment she hadn't experienced since her grandparents were alive. She hadn't seen much of them growing up, because her mother didn't like her in-laws, but they always hovered in the background of her life. They never forgot her birthdays, they paid for her braces and health insurance, and they socked away money in a college account for her. She didn't get to thank them, since they were both dead by the time she started college.

Sighing, she burrowed deeper into the crook of Rod's arm.

"You seriously considered giving up your grandfather's ranch to a lowlife like Bobby Jingo?"

"It's not mine to give up." But Rod had a point. Grandfather Ennis had hated scum like Bobby, and Dad seemed to surround himself with those kinds of people.

"If you got married to someone decent, it would be yours. You'd be fulfilling your grandfather's wishes, keeping the ranch in the family."

*Decent...* She lifted her head from his shoulder and rubbed her eyes, an idea niggling at the edges of her brain.

"What happens to the ranch if you don't get married?"

She pushed up from the church steps. "What?"

His brow furrowed. "What happens to the ranch if you don't get married?"

"I—I don't know." She began pacing on the wooden porch, avoiding stepping on the nails with her bare feet. "It goes to an associate or something."

She glanced at Rod, his long legs stretched in front of him, his arms folded across his chest. *It just might work.*

She could make it work. An arrangement with an honorable man would save her father, save her grandfather's ranch and save Jesse. She had to get that ranch.

Time to take action.

Standing up, Rod asked, "What's wrong with you?" He wedged his shoulder against a wood post and regarded her with his head tilted to one side, a lock of russet-gold hair falling over his eye.

He looked so damned sexy, it sealed the deal. Callie straightened her spine and stood on tiptoes in front of him. "I have an idea. It might sound crazy, but I think it'll work."

Rod narrowed his green eyes and his jaw tightened. Callie faltered, falling back on her heels. He didn't look so comforting right now, although the sex appeal rose as high as the church steeple above them.

"What kind of idea?"

Callie dragged in a deep breath and closed her eyes as she expelled it slowly. "Let's get married."

# Chapter Three

Callie's three little words punched him in the gut. He dug his shoulder into the post so he wouldn't tumble down the church steps.

"What?" His one syllable, which echoed in his own ears, forced Callie to jump back. He must've shouted.

Despite the almost-full moon that lit Hillsboro's main street, he couldn't make out the expression on her face. She was joking. She had that kind of sense of humor, one of the many things he liked about her.

He threw his head back and laughed at the moon.

"Rod." She shook his arm. "Rod, I'm not kidding."

Swallowing his next guffaw, he choked instead. Callie pounded him on the back. Working with clay or whatever material she used for sculpting gave her strength. Her pats felt like blows from a hammer.

"All right, all right." He straightened up and backed against the post. "That's a crazy idea. Insanity must run in your family."

"As someone once said, it not only runs, it gallops." She giggled, a nervous sound that resembled a squeak. "This may be crazy, but it'll work out for both of us."

"Exactly how will a marriage to a woman who has carloads of thugs chasing her around New Mexico and lunatic relatives help me?"

*The McClintock Proposal*

Rubbing her hands together, she resumed her pacing, obviously warming up to the idea. "Think about it. We get married, and then I get the title to the ranch. I can borrow against the equity or sell off a few acres and pay off my father's debts to Bobby Jingo."

"What do I get out of it?" *Other than the chance to claim this impossible, free-spirited, sexy woman as my own.*

"Money." She spread her arms in front of her, palms up, as if offering him the filthy lucre right here and now. "The ranch is huge. I can pay off Bobby, and there would still be plenty left over for you. You told me tonight how your ranch wasn't profitable. Why didn't you buy those horses in Austin? Too expensive?"

"I am *not* marrying a woman for money."

She dropped her hands and bunched the skirt of her dress in her fists. "You have an opportunity to save a man's life, not to mention *my* life, and all you can think about is your pride?"

The rabbit hole got deeper. How did he end up the bad guy? "Strangers don't run around getting married for money."

Her grimace melted into a smile, which washed over him, drowning his common sense.

"We're not strangers. We've known each other for about four hours, and we've experienced more drama than some couples do in a lifetime. Fear, terror and uncertainty draw people together."

He had to admit he'd opened up to this woman more than he did on a typical first date—most likely because he'd figured a woman fleeing from her wedding on a Honda 550 couldn't judge him. And this wasn't a first date. He uncrossed his arms and rolled his shoulders.

She continued, barely taking a breath. "People get

married for all kinds of crazy reasons—money chief among them."

Both of his brothers had married for love, but Rod never figured he'd find that with any woman. Being the oldest in the family, he remembered, more than his brothers, the cold indifference of their mother. He didn't want to risk winding up with that kind of family. So he took no risks at all.

"Look at me. I almost married someone horrible to get money to save my dad."

"And I'm much less horrible than Bobby Jingo?"

"Much less." She laughed and took his arm.

He glanced down at her deceptively fragile fingers, wrapped around his forearm. At least Callie put everything out there. She didn't have any ulterior motives, and there would be no expectations between them.

"What happens after you pay off your father's debts and buy me a few horses?"

She shrugged and the silky strap of her dress slid off her shoulder for about the hundredth time since he met her. This time he hooked a finger beneath the strap, his fingers skimming her soft skin as he righted it.

Drawing in a quick breath, she stepped back. "We partake of that other American institution—divorce."

"Alimony?"

"We'll work out a prenup. I don't want anything from you."

"Does your grandfather's will stipulate how long you have to enjoy your wedded bliss?"

She bit her lip and rolled her eyes to the sky. "At least two years. Why? Do you have plans?"

"Yeah, I think I'll have a few plans in the next two years."

"Do any of them involve a woman?"

"No."

"So what's the harm?" She grabbed his hands. "We stay married on paper for a few years, and then go our separate ways."

"I don't want people to think I married a woman to get her money."

"Don't look at it that way." She squeezed his hands and tilted her chin to gaze into his eyes. "You'd be saving my life, Rod, and my father's life. I need to find another studio and start working again. The money's there to sweeten the pot."

The pressure of her touch and the way her lips pouted inches from his own scrambled his senses. If he didn't marry her, how would she get the money? *He* couldn't loan it to her. Bobby Jingo would never stop pursuing her, but once she paid him off he'd leave her alone, especially if she were married…to someone else.

People married every day for far less noble causes than saving two lives.

He could keep his marriage a secret.

She'd go her way. He'd go his.

Maybe fate dropped a woman in a wedding dress on the side of the road for a reason.

*To hell with everything.*

Dipping his head, he took possession of those sweet lips. She dropped his hands, but he hitched an arm around her waist and dragged her closer, their bodies meeting along every line. She squirmed for a few seconds, slumped against him and then shimmied out of his grasp.

"Wh-what are you doing?"

"I'm kissing my bride-to-be."

Rod's words pierced through the cotton candy that had enveloped her from the moment his lips met hers. How could one kiss on the lips have such a monumental effect on every other part of her body? She felt…ravished. What would the rest of his anatomy do to her?

"Are you getting cold feet already?" His brows formed a V over his nose as his face gathered into a scowl.

"No. I'm thrilled. You've made me the happiest woman on earth." She twirled around the church porch until something sharp poked her heel. "Ow."

Lunging forward, he caught her in midspin. "What happened? Are you hurt?"

Oh yeah. She'd been right to play on his protective instincts. She hooked her injured foot behind her other ankle. "I think I got a sliver."

He swept her up in his arms, and then lowered himself onto the top step, sliding her bottom off his thigh so that her legs hung over his lap. "Which foot?"

"This one." She wiggled her left foot. "It's my heel."

He cupped her dirty foot in his hand as if he held a precious work of art. Then he dug into his pocket and withdrew a pocketknife.

She curled her toes. "I don't think it's big enough to cut out."

He snorted and plucked a pair of tweezers from the knife handle. "You *are* a city girl. Didn't you ever spend any time on your grandfather's ranch?"

"Not much. I moved around a lot with my mom." She squeezed her eyes shut and waited for the pain as the tweezers brushed her foot.

Several seconds later, Rod was massaging her foot. Her eyes flew open. "Do you think you're going to massage it out?"

Pinching the tweezers between his fingers, he held it up. "I already got the sliver out."

She hadn't felt a thing. Her husband-to-be had a gentle touch despite his calloused hands. How the hell had she gotten so lucky? Maybe the losing streak she'd been riding these past few years ran out of gas on I-25, along with that motorcycle.

"What's the plan?" Although she could sit here for the next three hours while Rod rubbed her foot, she had a wedding to attend.

"We get married."

"Now? It has to be past nine o'clock. We still have to get a marriage license."

"You almost got married in New Mexico. What do we need to get a license? Do we need a blood test?"

"We just need the license fee and a form of ID. No blood test, no waiting period. But I doubt if little ghost-town Hillsboro has a courthouse to get the license. Not to mention it's Saturday."

Rod slid the knife back into his pocket. "We'll have to wait anyway. You still have your driver's license?"

"Of course. How irresponsible do you think I am?" She shoved her hand into the fitted bodice of her dress and peeled her license from the side of her breast. "Ta-dah!"

He laughed. "You have a lot of tricks up your—or rather *down* your…a lot of tricks."

Hoisting her legs from his lap, he stood up and extended his hand to her.

She tucked her driver's license back into her strapless bra and grabbed his hand. "Where are we going?"

"Vegas, baby."

ROD SLEPT BESIDE HER in the truck, his breathing deep and even. He'd insisted on driving the first leg of their ten-hour trip while she napped in the passenger seat. When she woke up, he was sitting ramrod straight, his eyes glued to the road.

He'd broken their deal. They worked out that he'd drive the first five hours while she slept, and she'd take over the wheel for the second half of the journey. Instead, he'd let her sleep for over six hours. She practically had to wrestle the steering wheel away from him to drive her share.

His chivalry impressed her and made her feel like a gooey marshmallow inside. Nobody had ever looked out for her the way he had this crazy day. His every move, since he first pulled over on the side of I-25, had been to protect her.

Even though she'd used all her wheedling powers, common sense and logic, she still couldn't believe it when he agreed to her scheme. He'd admitted that he needed cash for his dude ranch, but she knew in her heart he'd based his decision on his desire to keep her safe. No, not desire, need. Something compelled him to perform good deeds.

She glanced at his handsome face, with its square jaw and broad cheekbones, one lock of hair curling over his eye. If he had such a burning passion to help women, why had matrimonial bliss eluded him so far? The man didn't even snore.

A glow, like a giant spaceship, arose from the desert landscape. She accelerated toward its exuberant embrace. So many people came to Vegas looking for salvation, her father among them; but for her, this neon paradise really did offer deliverance.

Twenty minutes later, she cruised off the highway toward the Vegas strip. She nudged Rod's shoulder with the heel of her hand. "We're here."

"Huh?" His head rolled to the side and he opened one eye.

"We're in Vegas. Wake up." Callie held her breath. Did his brief nap awaken him to the lunacy of their plan?

He rubbed his eyes and pinched the bridge of his nose. Then he cranked his head from side to side. "My neck's stiff."

No sign of regret yet. "Where to? Did the Marriage License Bureau give you directions when you called earlier?"

"It's on Clark Avenue."

Her pent-up breath escaped through her lips, as she sank against the leather seat. No regret at all. "Do you know how to get there?"

"No, but my GPS does." He reached beneath the passenger seat and pulled out a GPS, a black cord wrapped tightly around it.

"I didn't know you had one of those."

"I've made the trip to Austin a few times. Didn't need it for that drive." He plugged in the GPS and tapped the screen a few times. The monotone voice from the GPS intoned the first direction to Clark Avenue and the building that would seal her fate with this man for at least a few years.

When they walked inside the building, a blast of cold air greeted them, although the early morning temperature outside hadn't reached scorching levels yet.

They waited in a short line behind two other couples, nobody giving Callie's wedding dress a second glance. When they got to the counter, the clerk gave them each a form to complete. When they finished, they slid their forms, along with their driver's licenses, across the counter. Ten minutes later they walked out with their marriage license.

"Pretty simple for a momentous event."

"Is it a momentous event?" He raised an eyebrow, a half smile reaching his lips. "I thought we had a business arrangement."

"Of course we do. I meant a momentous event for other people." The words she uttered weighed down her heart. *For other people.* This kind of happiness swept others away, not her. And apparently not Rod.

"Let's get you some shoes for the occasion."

SEVERAL MINUTES LATER, he wheeled along the curved driveway of the Milano Hotel and Casino on the Strip.

A valet parking attendant helped her out of the truck as Rod plucked the parking claim ticket from another attendant. "Shops?"

"Level B, sir. When you enter the hotel, take the escalator to your right and go down one level."

Rod thanked the valet and ushered Callie into the hotel, the plush red carpet sinking beneath her bare feet. They entered a women's clothing store, open already at seven in the morning, or maybe it never closed.

Callie picked out a pair of off-white sandals with low heels. When the saleswoman began to take one of the sandals off her foot, Callie stopped her. "I'll wear them out."

Rod joined her at the counter, holding a gold band, ringed with small gemstones, between his thumb and forefinger. "Will this work as a wedding band?"

She took the ring from him and slipped it on her left ring finger. "Is it expensive?"

"It's cheap costume jewelry."

"Okay, it'll do." She held her left hand in front of her, admiring the sparkle of the fake gems. Her gaze collided with the bugged-out eyes of the saleswoman behind the counter.

"I-is that all, sir?"

"Add this." He slapped down a pack of spearmint gum.

"I don't know about you, but I haven't brushed my teeth in twenty-four hours."

"Ditto." Callie avoided looking at the saleswoman, whose mouth now resembled that of a gaping fish.

Rod handed over some plastic to pay for their purchases and asked, "Does the Milano have a wedding chapel?"

"Of course, and it's on this floor. When you leave the shop, turn to the right. Go to the end of the line of shops and turn left. The chapel is straight ahead."

As they left the shop, the woman called after them, "Congratulations and…good luck."

Their luck held. The chapel squeezed them in before the first scheduled wedding of the morning. Rod paid for the standard package, which included a small bouquet for her, a boutonniere for him, a commemorative photo and a witness.

Top-notch all the way. Callie grasped the bouquet in her hands, the cloying scent from the lilies making her woozy.

The clergyman smiled and began speaking about love, commitment and sacrifice. Callie nodded as if all those words applied to her and Rod. She swayed, and then dug the heels of her new sandals into the carpet.

Rod took her arm and grinned down at her. That grin didn't contain an ounce of hesitation or concern. Why should it? They had a deal. She'd promised to set him free once she met the conditions of her grandfather's will.

"Do you, Roderick McClintock, take this woman to be your lawfully wedded wife?"

"I do." Rod's voice sounded close to her ear, and she closed her eyes. The low timbre of his voice reverberated in her chest, unlocking dreams and desires she didn't realize she had.

McClintock. They didn't even know each other's last

names. Callie McClintock. Mrs. McClintock. Mrs. Roderick McClintock. Callie and Rod. Yeah, she'd promised to set him free…but she didn't want to.

"Do you, Callie…"

Her knees buckled as her world went black.

Callie sagged against him before crumpling into a heap at his feet. His mouth dry, he crouched beside her and called her name.

The clergyman joined him on the floor, fanning Callie's face with the marriage license. "Is she okay?"

Her golden lashes fluttered against her cheeks, and Rod blew out a breath. "Callie, are you all right?"

She struggled to sit up, and he wrapped an arm around her waist to help her, propping her against his thigh.

"Rod, I…we…"

"Shh. It's okay. We're going through with this." As he smoothed her hair back, he glanced at the clergyman. "She's nervous and hungry. We didn't stop for breakfast this morning, after a long drive. Can you finish the ceremony now?"

"O-on the floor?"

"Finish it."

The clergyman shot a worried look at Callie. "Miss?"

She nodded. "Let's get this done."

The clergyman shrugged. "I now pronounce you husband and wife. You may kiss the bride."

Rod planted his lips against Callie's forehead. He could save the real wedding kiss for later. He swept her up in his arms, dug in his pocket to tip the clergyman, and strode out of the chapel with his bride.

"Let's get breakfast."

"You can put me down now." She kicked her legs, with those strappy sandals on her feet.

"What happened in there?" He set her down but kept his arm around her, in case she decided to take another tumble. "Did you have second thoughts?"

Her blue eyes clouded over. "I didn't want to trap you into a situation you'd regret later. I realized how selfish I'd been."

"I agreed to help you." He gripped her shoulders, hooking his thumbs beneath the straps of her dress. "Once I commit to something, I see it through. And right now, I'm committed to finding breakfast."

THEY FOLLOWED THE HOTEL SIGNS to the buffet and parted company at their table.

Rod piled food onto a couple of plates, shook out his napkin, and ordered coffee from the waitress. He sipped the hot, mellow brew while he waited for Callie.

For a minute in the chapel, he thought she'd changed her mind and took a dive to opt out of the deal. Would he have cared? He would've dropped her off at the bus depot in Vegas and paid for a one-way ticket to L.A. Out of sight, out of mind.

*Yeah, right.*

He could no sooner put Callie…McClintock out of his mind than he could walk into that casino and drop a twenty at the blackjack table. Hell, he didn't even know her maiden name, but that didn't matter.

She was a McClintock now.

Callie returned to the table balancing two plates of food, one heaped with bacon, eggs and hash browns and one overflowing with a huge waffle topped with strawberries and whipped cream.

"Weddings give you an appetite?"

"Well, I did almost faint at the…er…altar."

They both dug into their food in silence, and Rod

downed three cups of coffee to combat the weariness that kept tugging at his eyelids. He figured they had another long drive ahead of them, to reach Callie's ranch in Wyoming.

Pushing back from the table, Rod tossed several dollars on the table. Callie scooped them up and counted out the eight dollars.

"Not enough?" Rod reached for his wallet.

"No. Very generous, considering we got our own food. I'm trying to keep track of how much I owe you, once I get my hands on some money."

"Don't worry about it. We're husband and wife, remember?"

She sucked in her lower lip and sighed. "I'm going to have to hit you up once more. I want to get out of this dress. Not taking a shower or brushing my teeth for twenty-four hours is bad enough."

He plucked some bills out of his wallet. "Buy yourself some clothes, a couple of toothbrushes and some toothpaste, and I'll roam the hotel hallways and filch some soap from a maid's cart. We'll clean up in one of the bathrooms before we take off."

A half-hour later—armed with two bars of soap and two towels tucked under his arm—Rod met Callie outside the shop where she'd bought her shoes. She handed him a toothbrush after squeezing some toothpaste onto the bristles, and he headed for the men's room. After he brushed his teeth and washed his face and neck, he hung the hotel towel over one of the stalls in the bathroom.

He caught his breath when Callie emerged from the ladies' room, her blond hair pulled back into a silky mane. The blue, flowered skirt brushed her slim calves, and the blue top matched the color of her eyes.

She looked pretty in the wedding dress, but it belonged to another time, another life.

The valet delivered his truck, and Rod pulled forward, idling at the end of the hotel driveway. "Okay, where to? Do you need to go straight to the ranch?"

"No." She tossed the wedding dress into the backseat. "I need to see my grandfather's attorney first."

"It's still Sunday. His office won't be open." Rod pulled out the GPS and secured it to the windshield. "And by the time we roll into Wyoming, it'll be close to ten o'clock at night."

She tilted her head, her ponytail slipping over her shoulder. "My grandfather's attorney isn't in Wyoming."

"I figured his attorney would be near the ranch." His fingers hovered over the GPS screen.

"It is, but the ranch isn't in Wyoming."

"You said he built a house on his ranch in Wyoming."

"Oh that. In all the excitement and prewedding jitters, I forgot to mention that he sold that original ranch and bought another one…in Colorado."

A prickling sensation attacked the back of his neck, and Rod rubbed it. "Colorado?"

"The ranch is in Colorado, and my grandfather's attorney is in Durango. So you see, we don't have that far to go. But you're right, his office will be closed on Sunday. So I guess it's to the ranch first. Un-unless you want to go to your home."

"Where is your ranch in Colorado?"

"It's outside of Durango in a former mining town, Silverhill."

Swallowing, Rod gripped the steering wheel with both hands, a low roar building in his ears. "Does the ranch have a name?"

"Yeah, the irony of it hit me on the road. You know how we were in Truth or Consequences?"

Rod nodded, his throat too tight to speak.

"Grandfather Ennis named his ranch Price Is Right. Isn't that a coincidence? Another game show? Maybe it was a sign."

"Price?"

"My last name." She snorted. "I know we didn't formally introduce ourselves but I'm, or rather I *was,* Callie Price."

The roar in his ears cascaded in a thunderous roll. Callie Price. Ennis Price, the eccentric old man who owned Price Is Right. The ranch right next to his own.

The ranch he just acquired by marrying old man Price's granddaughter.

# Chapter Four

The knuckles on the strong hands grasping the steering wheel bleached white, matching the line etched around her new husband's mouth. By revealing the name of the ranch, did she convince him that her relatives consisted of a bunch of howl-at-the-moon crazies?

Her fingers danced along the braided muscles of his forearm. "Don't worry. My family members aren't half as crazy as they seem. Besides, it's not as if we're going to procreate."

Not that she'd mind a few attempts at procreation with this hunk of sexy cowboy. She clenched her hands in her lap, trying to squelch the impure thoughts about her husband that galloped in her head.

Ignoring her attempt at a joke, Rod uncurled his hands from the steering wheel and flexed his fingers. "Silverhill, Colorado?"

"Near Durango." She tapped the GPS screen. "Should take us about nine hours. And don't go all macho on me. Let me take over the wheel when we're halfway there. I like to drive. Heck, I live in L.A. Our butts are practically glued to the seats of our cars."

That twisted a smile out of those sensuous lips, still tightly pursed. Maybe the food and coffee had restored him to his senses, and he was aware of the lunacy of this scheme.

*Tough.*

Rod's cheap wedding ring burned a circle around her finger, and she had their marriage license ready to wave in the face of her grandfather's attorney, Douglas Smyth Jr. Once Smyth stamped her name and Rod's on the title to Price Is Right, she'd sell off or borrow some money from the property, pay off Dad's debt to Bobby and hand over a tidy sum of cash to Rod for his part of the bargain.

Beyond that, she faced a murky future. She didn't have a clue what to do with a deserted ranch in Colorado. Maybe she'd sell the whole thing and return to L.A. She could start over with a new studio and buy a house in a good school district—prove to child services that she could provide a good home for five-year-old Jesse. That boy needed her as much as she needed him.

It had been over five months since she'd seen him, although she'd called him several times from New Mexico. He still remembered her, although he seemed distant, guarded, in their last conversation. She wouldn't desert him like everyone else had.

She sniffled. First things first. She popped the GPS off the windshield and entered Silverhill, Colorado, hesitating over the address entry. "Not sure what the address of the ranch is out there, but Silverhill's a small town. I'm sure someone can direct us to the ranch, once we roll in."

His jaw still tight, Rod started the engine of the truck and pulled away from the curb of the Milano. "About the ranch…"

Oh God, here it comes. The regret. The misgivings. The chivalry… The annulment?

"Stop. You saved me. Twice. You fought off Bobby's thugs and you agreed to marry me. You changed your plans and put your life on hold to help me—a complete stranger."

"But I…"

Callie held up her hands. "I know you're probably thinking people will peg you as a gold-digging cad, marrying me for money, but *I* know that's not true. And what do you care what the people in Silverhill, Colorado, have to say?"

"I do care. I know—"

"I understand your real reasons, and that's all that matters. You didn't know who I was and that I stood to inherit a bunch of land in Colorado when you rescued me at the side of the road. You didn't think there would be anything in it for you when you pummeled Bobby's guys and bloodied your own knuckles. And now here you are, married to someone you'd never laid eyes on, miles away from your home in…in…" She waved her hands around, not having a clue where he lived. "You will have earned every penny I can give you from the ranch."

She collapsed back in her seat, panting. "So don't get any ideas about ending this marriage. I need you. I need you to get that ranch, save my father and maybe even to save myself."

Ending on a sob, she allowed a single teardrop to tremble on the end of her lashes. As she slid her gaze in Rod's direction, the tear wobbled and then dripped onto her cheek.

A muscle in his jaw ticked as he glanced in her direction, his gaze scanning her face. "Why do you need saving, besides the obvious, and how's the ranch going to help?"

Drawing in a shaky breath, she tucked her hair behind one ear. "I traveled around a lot as a kid—when my parents were together, and with my mom after they split. My mom wasn't close to her own family, and, as I said before, she didn't like my father's parents. Sh-she had a problem with prescription drugs."

Rod shook his head, and she continued.

"We were living in California when it was time for me to go to college, so I ended up at UCLA for the in-state tuition and because they had a good fine arts department. I settled in L.A. by default. I don't have any roots there. I don't have any roots anywhere."

"Where's your mother?"

She curled her hands into fists. "She died of a drug overdose when I was in college."

He drew in a quick breath. "Sorry."

"The way she was going, it was bound to happen. She'd been skating on thin ice for a long time."

Rod drilled the road with a steely gaze, and Callie's heart flipped. She didn't want him to think she'd grow dependent on him or expect anything from him. He obviously didn't like that idea.

"Don't worry." She patted his muscled thigh. "With parents like I had, I've learned to depend on myself. That's why the ranch is important."

"Are you talking about the money it could bring?"

Callie clasped her hands between her knees and wiggled her toes in the new sandals. How could she explain her feelings to a man who had his own ranch somewhere? Probably had parents and extended family nearby. Probably had a life.

"It's more than just the money, although that will help my dad…and me. My grandparents built the ranch together, and my father never appreciated that. Grandfather Ennis left it to me on the condition of my marriage, hoping I'd establish my family there, put down some roots."

At Rod's sharp intake of breath, Callie dug her nails into the denim of his jeans. "Even if I keep the ranch, I can still pay you. In addition to the ranch, my grandfather owned a lot of land. I can sell off some of that property."

"It's not the money." Rod's hands clenched the steering wheel.

Uh-oh. All this talk of roots was scaring him.

"I don't need a husband to settle in at the ranch. Maybe I can set up a studio there, become part of a community. Surely there are people in Silverhill who remember my grandparents and my father. Perhaps they'll welcome me with open arms, accept me as a Price from Silverhill."

As she voiced her hopes to Rod, her pulse beat an excited rhythm through her veins. She'd been afraid to admit her expectations about the ranch, even to herself, but hearing them aloud breathed life into her dreams. The countryside and fresh air would benefit Jesse, too.

Rod snorted, popping her bubble. "You don't know small towns."

Callie drew her brows together, the fuzzy image of finding succor in the bosom of her adopted community fading fast. "Suspicious of outsiders, huh?"

"Yep."

"And an outsider is someone whose family hasn't lived there for a hundred years or more?"

"Pretty much."

"Are you accepted in your slice of small town heaven?" Mustn't be any single girls in that town, or they would've snapped him up years ago. She peered at him sideways through lowered lashes. Or he just liked the hard-to-get kind. She'd have to keep that in mind.

Not that she'd been exactly elusive in their brief history together.

He sawed his bottom lip with straight, white teeth. "Yeah, but it's not the cotton candy existence you've spun in your mind, Callie. Everyone knows your business, your family connections, your family's indiscretions." He grimaced. "We need to talk about your ranch and our situation."

"It's your ranch now." She yawned and reclined the seat back. "And I'm not up to talking."

She screwed her eyes shut, turning her face to the window. Those second thoughts were creeping into Rod's brain. She had to keep them at bay until the idea of their marriage grew on him, lodged itself in his mind as a done deal. Once they reached the ranch in Silverhill, he might just realize that nobody in his own small town need ever find out about his marriage of convenience. Then he could leave with his honor intact.

His intentions smacked of chivalry and nothing more.

She heard him inhale as if ready to unleash a torrent of words, and then soft, classical music filled the truck. Callie curled her legs beneath her, resting her cheek against her hand.

She'd never before encountered a man like Rod McClintock, and she feared she never would again. She intended to hold on to their brief married life with both hands. Maybe he'd discover something special in her, something that nobody else had ever seemed to find before, even her parents.

A girl could dream, couldn't she?

ROD CRUISED PAST THE FAMILIAR lights of Durango on his way to Silverhill and glanced at the sleeping woman beside him. Her blond hair spread like a silky fan across her cheek, golden strands clinging to her parted lips.

He cursed under his breath, shifting the toothpick from

one side of his mouth to the other. He'd have to break the news to her tonight. The news that the selfless savior she thought she'd married was actually her next door neighbor, with a whole lot to gain from his recent marriage.

She'd have to believe he had no idea he'd married Callie Price, old Ennis Price's granddaughter. What stroke of crazy coincidence had placed Callie on the highway precisely at the moment he was driving by? Precisely at the moment when he'd been wondering what the hell he was going to do about his ranch.

Maybe that fairy godmother had dropped her in his lap.

He snapped the toothpick in two and then dropped it into the cup holder. If he had a fairy godmother, she'd been on hiatus for a long time.

He'd wanted to tell Callie the truth as soon as he discovered her identity, but she kept cutting him off. Then, when she started to cry, she seemed so alone. She didn't even have a mother. He hadn't wanted to create any more anxiety for her.

Hell, she might just believe he'd known all along and accuse him of marrying her to get the ranch. That's why he had to tell her as soon as they got to the Price Is Right ranch and he got her settled.

He turned off the highway onto a smaller road that would take them past the Ute reservation and bypass town on the way to Callie's ranch. Even though it was almost nine o'clock at night, Rod didn't want to risk running into any of his acquaintances, least of all his brother, the sheriff.

He'd let her drive after they stopped for some lunch, but then he practically had to wrestle the steering wheel from her to drive the last leg into Silverhill. He'd wanted to avoid having her drive down the center of Main Street and pulling over to ask directions from someone who happened to know him. Of course, taking the back roads to the ranch would seem odd, too, so when Callie fell asleep, the tension in his muscles loosened.

Must be that fairy godmother again.

After they sped past the reservation, Rod took two more turns before his truck rumbled up the country road toward the Price Is Right ranch. Over the years, Price's estate had kept people employed at the ranch to perform some basic maintenance. Currently, a couple looked after the ranch. They stopped in once or twice a month. Rod hoped their visit didn't coincide with the caretakers'.

"Callie?"

She stirred and shifted, her long hair flowing like a waterfall over her face. Rod hooked a finger along the length of her silken strands, sweeping them off her cheek. Like shards of gold, her hair caught on the rough pads of his fingers.

"Callie?"

Murmuring, she lifted her head and blinked. She massaged the back of her neck. "Huh?"

"We're here."

"We're home?"

A fist clutched his heart. Did she crave a home to call her own so badly, she'd grab at any straw, no matter how flimsy? He didn't think she'd find that home in Silverhill.

"Do you know how to get into the ranch?"

"Dad told me the caretaker leaves a key on the porch." Callie rubbed her eyes and peered out the window. "Did you have any trouble finding the ranch?"

"Nope." He wheeled in front of the sagging porch and cut the engine. The headlights from his truck went out, leaving them in murky darkness, relieved only by the glow from the moon, shadowed in clouds. The caretakers couldn't put a porch light on a timer?

He clicked on the truck's lights, bathing the porch in their yellow glow. "I'll leave the lights on while you get the key."

Callie shoved her feet back into her sandals and pushed out of the car. The headlights picked up her slight figure as she charged up the two porch steps. She staggered and squealed, throwing her arms out to the sides of her body as she lurched forward.

His heart pounding, Rod flung open the car door and stumbled out. "What's wrong?"

"I stepped in a hole." She pointed down. "This porch is falling apart."

"Are you okay?" Leaving the car door open, he strode up to the house. "Let me get the key."

She glanced at his cowboy boots, and then her gaze tracked up the length of his large frame. "I think you're more likely to fall through this rotting wood than I am. The key is just under this planter, at least I hope so."

Callie pulled her foot out of the gaping hole in the porch. Bending forward, she tilted back a clay pot and reached beneath it with one hand, fingers splayed. She swept the surface beneath the pot. "It's not here."

"Could it be under another planter?"

She glanced back, the headlights catching the golden glints of her hair as it fell over her shoulder. "Do you see another planter?"

He hunched his shoulders while twisting his head from side to side. He had to admit, the caretakers left the place pretty barren. "We're going to have to break in."

"That's just great. I don't even own the place yet."

"You're going to start standing on ceremony now?"

She grinned. "You have a point."

He held out his hand to help her off the rickety porch. As she gripped his fingers, he pulled her forward. She flew off the porch and into his arms.

"Whoa. You don't know your own strength." She tilted back her head, laughing, but she didn't make a move.

He tightened one arm around her slender waist and traced a finger along her jaw. "You're a wisp of a thing—with the grip of a wrestler."

She tilted her head back farther, the ends of her hair tickling his forearm. "It's from working with clay. I'm stronger than I look, Rod."

"I hope so."

Her jaw tightened as she broke away from his embrace and took two steps back. "How do you propose we break in?"

He had a knack for ending the moment. She'd meant to reassure him she wouldn't be hanging on to him like a drowning woman, and he'd slapped her down. Who was he kidding anyway?

He'd always been a sucker for drowning women.

Rubbing the stubble on his chin that was fast becoming a beard, he stepped back and scanned the front of the house. Lots of windows, but they didn't need to break any in the front. "Let's go around to the side."

He reached for her hand, but she shook him off and strode ahead. She stumbled in the darkness and muttered a curse. "Don't you have a flashlight in your truck?"

"No, but my eyes are adjusting, and if those clouds shift to the right, we'll have enough light to break a window." As if on cue, the clouds parted and the moon cast light on the path in front of them

Gasping, Callie came to a sudden stop and Rod plowed into her back, almost knocking her off her feet. For the second time in five minutes, he had his hands encircling her waist.

He peered over her shoulder as she pointed to the window, its jagged edges gleaming in the faint moonlight.

"It's already broken. What are the chances of that?" She extended her index finger and tapped at a piece of glass pointing down like an arrow.

"Be careful." He cinched his hand around her wrist, pulling her back. "Don't cut yourself."

"What kind of caretakers run the place?" She leaned forward, tilting her head to look at the rim of the window. "I think we can unlock it."

"We?" He tucked her behind his back and reached into the gaping hole. He tapped his fingers along the sash until they stumbled across the lock, and then he twisted it to the left. "I think I got it."

He shoved the window open, and Callie tapped him on the shoulder. "Let me climb in. I'll come around the front and open the door."

"I can fit through. And there's probably glass on the other side. I don't want you to cut yourself."

She wedged her hands on her hips. "I thought you wanted me to fend for myself? Besides, I don't think I can give you a boost over that ledge."

He opened his mouth to protest, but she spun toward the window and grasped its ledge. "Come on. Give me a lift."

Placing his hands on her hips, Rod hoisted her up and she ducked into the house headfirst and disappeared with a flutter of sandaled feet.

He cupped his hand and yelled, "Watch out for the glass on the floor. I'm going around to the front. I hope you don't need a key to open the deadbolt from the inside."

She called back to him in an unintelligible voice, and he made his way back to the front of the house. Just as he killed the headlights on his car, a warm, yellow glow appeared from the house.

Rod grabbed the cooler from the backseat, where they'd stashed sandwiches for later, and slammed the car door. He vaulted up the porch steps, avoiding the broken boards, and rattled the doorknob.

"Can you open the front door?"

The only answer he received was a piercing scream.

# Chapter Five

Vaguely aware of Rod banging on the front door and calling her name, Callie clamped her hands over her mouth as she stared at the white froth spilling over the coffee table.

Her bridal veil.

She crept toward the veil, as if expecting it to take flight around the room. She poked at it with her toe. It whispered, and a little more of it slipped off the table.

How the heck did it get here? The last time she saw this piece of confection, she'd been getting ready to hop on a motorcycle in Las Cruces.

Clutching her stomach, she spun around, squinting into the darkness of the back rooms, and then shifting her gaze to the staircase. Suddenly, she no longer felt like fending for herself.

And why should she? She had a cowboy outside, ready to break down the door and come to her rescue.

She stumbled toward the pounding, her heart mimicking its beat. With shaky fingers, she turned the dead bolt and twisted the door handle. Rod almost knocked her over as he charged into the room, dropping a cooler on the floor.

"What happened?"

She pointed an unsteady finger at the veil. "That's mine. I left it in New Mexico before I ditched the wedding."

In two long strides, Rod reached the veil and scooped it up with one hand. He crumpled it in his fist, and then grabbed her hand. "I need some backup before I search the house."

"Before *we* search the house. I'm not waiting anywhere by myself."

After flicking on the porch light and a few more lamps, Rod stalked back to his truck. Callie kept a tight hold on his hand, her fingers stiff and cold despite the warmth of the evening. He had to shake her off to retrieve his gun from the truck, and when he turned back toward the house, she hooked her fingers in the back pocket of his jeans.

He searched the big ranch house with Callie trailing behind him, occasionally stepping on his heels or stumbling into his back. She eventually loosened her stranglehold on his pocket and peeked under beds and threw open closet doors.

After they gave the house the once-over, they returned to the front room and Rod checked the locks on the door and twitched aside the curtain on the window to peer outside.

"Why do you think Bobby Jingo came all the way up here from New Mexico? Does he think he's going to force you into marriage?"

Her brows collided over her nose. "I don't know. I'm sure he's mad as hell that I left him at the altar, torpedoing his plans for this ranch, but he has to know I'm going to pay my dad's debts."

"Maybe not." Rod still gripped his gun, even though they'd turned up nothing in the house. "He doesn't know you're married now. Why would he even think you hightailed it to the ranch instead of back to L.A., after skipping the wedding—to him. Maybe he came to the ranch to see if he could take something of value. Can you tell if anything is missing or disturbed?"

She folded her arms, chewing her bottom lip. "Disturbed? Some of the artwork around the house is pretty disturbing, but other than that, I couldn't say. It's been a long time since I've been to Colorado."

Rod settled his gun on top of the veil, an incongruous image if he ever saw one. "You've been here before?"

"A long time ago." She waved her arm around the room. "I was probably eight or nine. Grandpa Ennis tried to put me on a horse, and I didn't tell him I was terrified. I just wanted to please him so he'd invite me back."

ROD WEDGED A SHOULDER against the edge of the window and gazed outside, but instead of seeing the room behind him reflected in the darkness, he saw a sunny day on a riding trail with his brothers. His youngest brother, Rafe, had rushed ahead as usual, startling a rider coming from the other direction.

A little girl, not much older than Rafe, squealed as her horse bucked, tossing her into the air, long blond pigtails flying behind her. Rafe doubled over with laughter, and Ryder, Rod's middle brother, began explaining to the girl what she should've done to stay in her saddle.

Her rescue rested with Rod. He slid out of his saddle and rushed to the girl, now lying flat on her back, large blue eyes gazing up at the equally blue sky.

He bent over her, his head blocking the sun, casting her face in shade. "Are you okay? My brother's an idiot."

Her eyes focused on his face and she grinned. "I meant to do that. But your brother's still an idiot."

One of the first times in his young life Rod ever admired a girl.

CALLIE SIGHED BEHIND HIM. "I didn't find out until later. She never told me about the invitations."

"What did you say?" Rod turned and looked into those same blue eyes, a little cloudier, but still as beautiful as he remembered.

"My mother. My grandparents did invite me back to the ranch, but my flakey mom rejected their invitations on my behalf. My grandparents objected to my mom's dependence on prescription drugs, and they let her know about it. All those years, I thought I had disappointed my grandparents in some way—that they didn't want me back."

She traced the handle of his gun with her fingertip. "Will you teach me how to shoot one of these?"

"You're not still depressed about those missed invitations, are you?" He raised his brows.

She laughed. "Don't worry. I won't do anything desperate. That's all in the past. I'm here now, and ready to take Silverhill by storm."

He touched his finger to her nose. He still saw that little girl on the horse trail trying to put on a brave face. "I hope your expectations aren't too high."

"I've already had a lifetime of tempering my expectations, Rod. You don't have to warn me."

*Yeah, right.* Callie didn't strike him as a weary cynic. He hoped she wasn't setting herself up for a big disappointment. The folks of Silverhill could be an insular group of people. And he could tell her all about them.

Jerking his thumb toward the upended cooler on the floor, he said, "Let's eat those sandwiches we bought earlier, after we board up that broken window. And then we need to talk."

She made a face. "Do you think we'll find a hammer and nails in that tool shed by the side of the house?"

"I'm counting on it."

AFTER THEY NAILED SOME PLYWOOD over the gaping window, they returned to the front room. Rod righted the cooler and flipped it open. He dug out the two sandwiches wrapped in brown paper, and shoved the veil aside on the coffee table to make room for dinner.

Callie's laughter bubbled. "First class all the way. I'll check the fridge. Maybe the caretakers left something from their last visit."

She emerged from the kitchen clinking two bottles of beer together. "Eureka. I'm beginning to like those caretakers, even if they did abscond with the key to the front door."

She sank into the sofa next to him and unwrapped the sandwiches, while he twisted the caps off the beer bottles.

Propping up her feet on the table, she grabbed a bottle and chugged a quantity of beer, then wiped her mouth with the back of her hand. "Ahh, I needed that."

Rod quirked a brow. "Any more of those in there or do you want mine, too?"

She nudged the bottle in his direction with her foot. "A six-pack. Hell, that's four more than I need to get buzzed."

"You planning to get buzzed?" He took a big bite of his slightly soggy sandwich and washed it down with a gulp of beer. He might need to get her tipsy before he broke the news to her.

*Coward.*

"I'd never get drunk on my wedding night." She tapped her feet together. "Bad form."

She downed the rest of her beer and hiccupped.

"I think you'd better get something in your stomach besides alcohol." Rod shoved a sandwich toward her. "'Cuz I have something to tell you."

"Save it." She opened her sandwich and picked off the wilted lettuce. "Can I enjoy just one night of wedded bliss before facing my problems?"

He toyed with the sandwich paper. His news would definitely present her with another set of problems, but she had a right to know. "You need to hear this, Callie, but it can wait until we finish eating."

"Good." While she chewed, her brow furrowed. "Do you think Bobby left Silverhill when he didn't find what he was looking for?"

Rod shrugged and scratched a line through the label on the bottle with his fingernail. "Who said he didn't find what he was looking for? You don't know if anything is missing. Would your father know?"

"I doubt if Dad would know. But maybe Smyth, the attorney, would know."

Rod almost choked on the last bite of his sandwich. "Smyth?"

She snorted. "Yeah, should be Douglas Smyth the third, or something equally snooty to match the name, but he's only a junior."

Rod scraped off another line of label and bit the inside of his cheek. It figured that old man Ennis would hire Doug Smyth as his attorney. All the ranchers used Smyth, including him.

"Callie…"

She yawned and curled her legs beneath her. "Could you get me another beer, Rod?"

He blew out a breath and pushed up from the sofa.

Maybe they both needed another beer to get through this conversation. "Sure."

He swept the trash from the table and carried it into the kitchen. He didn't see a trash can, so he rummaged through a few cupboards, looking for a paper bag. Nothing. He crumpled the sandwich wrappers on the counter and retrieved two more beers from the fridge. Nothing remained on the refrigerator shelves except two final bottles of beer—enough to send Callie over the edge of reason—and a lonely can of pop.

"You're going to need to go grocery shopping tomorrow morning." He returned to the front room. Callie had her head tilted back against a cushion, her eyes closed, her hair fanning around her like a halo.

"Do you still want the beer?"

She opened one eye. "Uh-huh."

He placed the bottle on the table in front of her. "I'm going out to my truck to get the rest of my stuff and a paper bag for the trash. I need my cell phone charger, too."

"You don't have a cell phone." She hunched forward and took a small sip from the bottle.

"Oh, yeah. But I do have a toothbrush—two toothbrushes. I'll be right back. Then we talk." He jogged down the front steps and unlocked his truck. He pulled out the bag with the toiletries they'd bought in Vegas, and his briefcase containing the information on the horses in Texas. Seemed a million light years ago.

He could have enough money to buy those horses now—if he planned to hold Callie to their deal. But he had no intention of doing that. He'd stay married to her long enough so that she could keep her ranch and her money, and then they could start all over again…as neighbors.

But he had to tell her the truth first, or there would be no starting over with her.

The beads on Callie's wedding dress glittered and winked, almost mocking him. He'd finally gotten married, and it was all a fake. His bride would leave him even faster than his mother left her family. But he knew that going in. That's what made it easy to walk down that aisle. No surprises. No wondering and waiting when she'd make her move.

He hauled out the gown and tossed it over his shoulder. Time to let Callie in on the big joke—she'd married a McClintock from Silverhill.

He trudged up the steps and kicked the door wide. "Thought I'd better bring in the wedding dress, too. Who knows? Maybe you can get it cleaned up and repaired and wear it to your real wedding some day."

He dropped his load in the nearest chair and turned to Callie. Still curled up on the sofa, she had her head resting against a cushion on the arm. Her long hair streamed over her face, strands lifting and falling with every breath she took. Sound asleep.

"Callie?"

She murmured and threw an arm over her head.

Rod blew out a long breath and slid a crocheted afghan from the back of the chair. He adjusted the cushion beneath Callie's head and tucked the afghan around her body, his fingers trailing over her soft calves. He leaned forward and kissed her temple, soft tendrils of her hair tickling his lips.

His game of truth or consequences would have to wait until morning.

CALLIE STUFFED THE MARRIAGE license into the glove compartment of Rod's truck. Then she cranked on the engine and punched Smyth's address, which she'd found in the phone book, into the GPS. As she cruised down the driveway, she glanced at the house in her rearview mirror.

She couldn't believe something finally belonged to her...well, her and Rod. The knowledge encased her heart in a warm glow. Would Jesse like it here? She hoped he'd get a chance to discover for himself.

She noticed a small, squat building to the right of the house, which she'd missed last night in the darkness. She could rip off the roof, install some skylights and turn it into a studio. Maybe she could do the work herself, if she could get a little more money out of the ranch after paying off Bobby...and Rod.

She didn't want to disturb Rod this morning. He couldn't have enjoyed a good night's sleep stretched out on the living room floor, a tiny blanket leaving his feet exposed. He could've slept in a real bed in one of the bedrooms. During their search of the house, she'd noticed several made-up beds. Maybe the sheets had been musty or something.

Or maybe Rod just wanted to be close to her because of the break-in.

That knowledge increased the warmth around her heart. She didn't want to explore the heat it generated in other parts of her anatomy. Rod had signed up for a marriage of convenience, nothing more.

Twenty minutes later, she took the off-ramp leading to Durango and followed the polite voice of the GPS lady to Smyth's office on West Twelfth Street. She pulled to a stop around the corner, across from a park.

The small shopping center down the street made her mouth water. Hopefully, Smyth could give her an advance on her inheritance, so she could buy some clothes to get her through the next week or two. Then Dad could send her things up here, or maybe even bring them in person.

A small knot tightened in her belly. The ranch didn't have phone service, but she could've tried to call Dad sooner. Since Bobby and his entourage had driven up to the ranch, maybe he'd left Dad alone.

Her gaze tracked along the edge of the park and the sidewalk lining the street. Where had Bobby gone after he broke into the ranch?

On the morning of her wedding to him, she'd discovered he didn't lose any money due to a business deal with Dad. How could she have misjudged him so completely? He seemed like a nice guy, and wasn't too bad on the eyes either. He'd turned out to be a bookie—no surprise there, given Dad's proclivities. She should've figured that out sooner.

What she'd hoped would be a sure path to adopting Jesse, an instant father, turned into a nightmare. After investigating Bobby's background, the adoption agency would've snatched Jesse from her arms in under a second.

Even worse, Bobby had aspirations beyond two-bit loan sharking, which made him too dangerous to dismiss lightly. If Bobby just wanted Dad to repay the debt, Callie could've washed him out of her hair in a week. But if the conversation she'd overheard that morning was any indication, Bobby had bigger plans for the ranch and her money. And she might have a tougher time getting rid of him.

She'd need Rod McClintock for that job.

Sighing, she hopped from the truck and, clutching her marriage license, smoothed her wrinkled skirt over her thighs. She checked the addresses on the buildings lining

Twelfth Street and pushed through the glass doors of a small, two-story stucco structure.

She ran a finger down the glass-encased building directory until she found the law office of Smyth and Sons. She followed the arrow to office 128 and eased open the door.

A dark-haired receptionist with cherry-red lips smiled from behind her desk. "Jerry or Junior?"

"E-excuse me?"

"Do you have an appointment with Jerry Smyth or Doug?" She swiveled her wheeled chair in front of a computer screen and tapped the keyboard.

"I'm here to see Douglas Smyth—Junior—but I don't have an appointment." She didn't have a phone, a car or a purse. She sure as hell didn't have an appointment.

The receptionist bunched up her red lips and tapped a few more keys. "He might be able to squeeze you in before his first appointment at ten o'clock." She picked up a telephone receiver. "What's your name?"

Callie straightened her shoulders. "I'm Callie Price, Ennis Price's granddaughter. Actually, I'm Callie Price McClintock now. That's why I'm…"

She broke off as the receptionist dropped the receiver. "Callie Price M-McClintock?"

"That's right." Callie drew her brows together. Had Dad already notified Smyth that she'd be marrying Bobby Jingo? "I just got married, and I have some business with Mr. Smyth."

"Of course. I'll find out if he can see you now." She picked up the receiver and pressed a button. "Doug, Callie Price is here to see you. Ten o'clock. Yes, but…"

She directed a tight smile at Callie and replaced the receiver. "He's going to squeeze you in."

A door to the right of the lobby burst open, and a short,

muscularly built man charged through, hand extended. "Callie? Great to finally meet you. Your father called several weeks ago to tell me about your engagement. Congratulations. I've been expecting you."

"Nice to meet you, too."

As Smyth gripped her hand in a hard handshake, he tugged her toward his office. That explained the receptionist's surprise. She expected a different last name.

The receptionist cleared her throat. "You knew about the wedding? Why didn't anyone tell me?"

Smyth aimed a scowl over Callie's shoulder at his office worker. "Tanya, maybe Mrs. Jingo would like some coffee."

Callie shook her head at Tanya's flushed face. She'd have some explaining to do, but she wasn't about to do it with the gaping Tanya looking on. "Nothing for me, thanks."

Tanya had stood up, placing her palms flat on her desk. "But she's…"

Smyth cut her off and ushered Callie into his office. "Hold all my calls, Tanya, but buzz me when my ten o'clock shows up, if Callie and I are still busy."

He snapped the door shut and rolled his eyes at Callie. "I apologize for my receptionist's unprofessionalism. Of course, we don't discuss our clients' business with the office staff."

Gesturing toward a leather chair across from his desk, he said, "Please have a seat."

Callie placed the marriage license on the desk and smoothed her palm across the top, trying to iron out the wrinkles. "I brought the marriage license as proof, in case you need it."

Smyth crouched beside a four-drawer filing cabinet and slid open the bottom drawer. "Yes, we'll need to make a copy and add it to the file. Your grandfather hired my father to see to his affairs and, of course, this trust. My father retired four years ago, but he handled most of the ranchers in this area. I don't know if you know the history of Silverhill, Callie, but most of the ranching families got their wealth through the silver mines. Your grandfather was a relative newcomer."

Callie clutched the arms of the chair. Great. If the residents of Silverhill had considered her grandfather Ennis a newcomer, they'd have no time for his granddaughter, who'd made all of three visits here.

She uncurled her hands and folded them on top of the license. "I don't really know the history of Silverhill, but I'd like to learn about it. I—I might have plans to settle here."

"And your new husband?" Smyth emerged from the filing cabinet clutching a thick manila folder. "Would he be willing to settle here?"

Callie had no intention of getting into any details with the attorney. The nature of her nuptials might render the entire agreement null and void, and she couldn't afford that right now.

She pasted on a smile that hurt her cheeks. "We're discussing it now."

"Wonderful." Smyth dropped the cumbersome file onto the desk with a plop. "There are quite a few papers I need to review with you, and quite a few papers for you to sign. Your grandfather left a variety of assets in addition to the ranch."

"He did?" Her eyes widened. Bobby's desperation to marry her clicked into focus a little more.

"Ennis Price was…eccentric. Your father must have told you about that. Your grandfather also lived very frugally despite his extensive wealth."

"Extensive wealth? He never shared any of that wealth with my father, his only son."

Smyth cleared his throat. "Yes, well, Ennis didn't much approve of your father's lifestyle."

"You mean his gambling." Callie's jaw hardened. She didn't much approve of Dad's lifestyle either. Grandpa Ennis knew what he was doing. Dad could've blown through a fortune over the years. A fortune that now belonged to her.

"Just show me where and what to sign, and maybe I can get an advance on some of the money. I…uh, lost my wallet."

Frowning, Smyth stopped shuffling papers. "That could be a problem, since I need to see your driver's license."

"Oh, I have that." Callie stood up and reached into the pocket of her skirt.

"Excellent. After signing the papers, you can go right to the Bank of Colorado and withdraw funds yourself." He tapped his pen on top of the stack of papers he had prepared for her. "However, we will need to get your husband in here to sign the deed of trust to the ranch. The money and accounts are all yours, but I'm afraid your husband owns half of the ranch and the surrounding property." Smyth hunched his shoulders. "I never liked that part of the agreement."

Callie blew out a breath. She could trust Rod, but she suspected Bobby knew a lot more about the terms of this agreement than she did. What would he have done to her to get the rest of the money, once they were married?

She suppressed a shiver. "I know about the ranch. Dad explained the conditions of the trust to me."

Smyth rubbed his hands together and turned the papers toward her in a neat pile, dropping a pen on top. "I've put an X beside each line you need to sign. Are you sure you wouldn't like some coffee or water?"

"No, thank you." Callie picked up the heavy pen and positioned the tip at the first line. "I suppose I have to sign my married name now."

"That's right." Smyth smiled. "Don't worry. My wife had to sign so many documents when we first got married, she got used to it."

Callie started signing as Smyth's phone buzzed.

He glanced at the red light. "My next appointment is here, but take your time. We're almost done. Then you can set up another appointment with Tanya for you and your husband, and we can go over the fine points of the trust. As I mentioned, your grandfather had some odd ideas."

Callie clamped her lips together as she scanned the next document, before signing with a shaking hand. Yeah, some odd ideas—and piles of assets. She was freakin' rich. Did Dad even know Grandpa Ennis had all this dough? He must have, and he must have clued in Bobby. When she'd overheard Bobby's ambitions regarding her property, it hadn't made much sense. Now it did.

She dropped the pen and flexed her fingers. "All done." She peeled a card from the glass top of the desk. "I just need to show this to the bank to transfer the account to my name and withdraw some cash?"

"That's right." Smyth tapped the stack of papers on his desk to straighten the edges. "They'll probably have you fill out some forms to get an ATM card, and there's a safety deposit box there as well. Now, I'll just have Tanya make a copy of these and your marriage license, and you can be on your way back to that new husband of yours."

Callie shoved the license toward him, and he glanced at it while he settled it on top of the other papers.

His eyebrows shot up to his bald pate and he dumped

the license off the papers. His gaze tracked down the first page to her signature, and then he began flipping through each page, creating a flurry of paper on his desk.

Callie gripped the arms of the chair as she watched him. Okay, so he knew she hadn't signed "Callie Jingo." Would that make a difference? Maybe she could just tell him Dad had the wrong name of her betrothed. That's something Dad could forget.

After shuffling through each paper, he jerked his head up. "McClintock? You married Rod McClintock?"

*Bluff your way through it, Callie.* She tilted her head and smiled. "Yes, Rod McClintock is the name of my husband. I'm Callie McClintock."

"How did you meet Rod?"

Her smile faltered as she dug her nails into the leather. Was he going to demand proof that they consummated the union, too? "I...we met in New Mexico. At a—uh—horse show. I like horses."

Smyth smacked the desk and she jumped. "I'll be damned. What a coincidence."

"Coincidence?"

"What a coincidence you and Rod met down in New Mexico. I know he's been down there a few times looking at horses."

"You do?" Her voice squeaked, and she didn't even realize she'd jumped from her chair, until it fell over with a thud.

This time Smyth's smile faltered. "As his attorney and friend, I know a few of Rod's plans."

Callie felt the blood drain from her face, leaving her light-headed. She swayed. "Attorney? Friend? You know my husband, Rod?"

Smyth blinked his eyes several times, resembling some

bald-headed bird. "Of course I know Rod. Everyone knows Rod. He's one of the McClintocks from Silverhill. And he owns the ranch right next to yours."

# Chapter Six

Rod stretched and rolled to the side, banging his knee against the coffee table. Yawning, he massaged his tight neck. Miserable night. He could've nabbed one of the beds upstairs, but he didn't want to leave Callie alone down here, and he didn't want to wake her.

Bobby Jingo could've been waiting in the shadows somewhere for a chance to snatch his bride.

*His* bride.

Rod hitched up to a sitting position, his flimsy blanket sliding off his shoulders. *Helluva way to spend your wedding night, McClintock.*

Callie had already vacated the sofa, folding the Afghan neatly over the back. Maybe she snuck off to one of the beds in the middle of the night.

He pushed to his feet and stretched again before making for the staircase. Judging by the light shafting through the drapes, he'd slept in late; but if Callie needed to sleep even later, he'd let her. He could run into town and pick up a couple of breakfasts at the Miner's Café.

He crept up the stairs and peeked into the first room, and then the next, and the next, and the next—until he ran out of rooms.

"Callie?"

The bathroom doors yawned open, the rooms all empty.

He called her name again and jogged downstairs. Had she gotten the jump on him and gone out for breakfast first?

Then he spotted a single sheet of white paper on the coffee table, beneath a beer bottle. His gut lurched. He grabbed the note and scanned the contents, crumpling it in his fist when he finished reading.

Callie probably knew the true identity of her new husband by now.

Rod cursed as he yanked on his boots and charged out of the house. Stumbling into the driveway, he looked around wildly for his truck, his fingers laced through his hair. She took his truck.

He'd call Rafe for a ride into Durango. He patted his shirt pocket, and then howled at the empty yard. She took his phone.

He knew the phone lines in the house didn't work. They'd tried them last night. His own ranch, and his motorcycle, lay almost two miles west of Price Is Right, but he had to get to Durango. If Callie couldn't get in to see Doug Smyth, Rod still had a chance to spring the news on her. This had to come from *him*.

He latched the gate to the drive behind him and set off down the road that led to his ranch. He walked for five minutes before a squad car roared toward him, lights revolving.

The car squealed to a stop just yards in front of him, and his brother, Rafe, stuck his head out the window. "Where the hell have you been? Did you walk back from New Mexico?"

Rod hadn't been this happy to see his youngest brother in a long time. He grabbed the handle of the passenger side door and yanked it open.

"Just in time…for once. I need a ride into Durango."

Rafe tipped his hat back on his head. "Durango?

Where's your truck? I just went to the ranch to see if you wanted to have breakfast. I thought you were coming home the day before yesterday."

Rod pounded the dash. "Just drive."

"How do you know I don't have important police business to conduct?"

"You told me you were on your way to have breakfast."

Rafe accelerated and put his lights on, pointing to the roof of the car. "I can get you there faster this way."

"Using your authority for personal gain?"

"Are you in a hurry or not?"

"Hurry."

Rafe slowed the car and waved to a couple walking on the shoulder of the road. "I suppose it wouldn't do me any good to ask you what's going on."

"Nope."

They drove in silence as Rafe wended his way around the outskirts of Silverhill and hit the highway toward Durango.

"Dana wants you over for dinner on Friday. She has a friend down from Denver, works in the behavioral sciences division of the FBI. Thinks you two might hit it off."

A bead of sweat rolled down Rod's temple and dripped into his ear. At least his marriage to Callie would save him from the awkward blind dates his sisters-in-law insisted on engineering for him.

"I'll pass."

"You look like crap. She probably wouldn't like you anyway. Are you growing a beard?"

Rod grunted and slid lower in his seat.

He snapped at every question Rafe asked, finally wearing him down into a companionable, morose silence. Rafe had always occupied the role of the social animal in the McClintock family—had inherited most of the charm, too.

Rafe would have no problem convincing Callie their meeting had been a coincidence.

As Rafe cruised into Durango, he glanced at Rod. "Are you going to tell me where to drop you, or are you just going to jump out of the moving car?"

"Take me to Smyth's office."

Rafe pulled up to the curb, and Rod spotted his truck across the street. Maybe Callie hadn't been able to see Doug yet. "This is good. Thanks for the ride. Tell Dana I'll take a rain check on dinner—without the extra guest."

Rod jumped out of the car and started toward Doug's office building, when a flurry of activity and color caught his attention. He peered down the street at a petite blonde, bulging shopping bags swinging from her arms.

He shoved his hands in his pockets, legs apart, waiting for…whatever. A big pair of dark sunglasses hid Callie's eyes, but he knew she'd spotted him by the hitch in her stride.

Rod lifted a hand in a wave as Callie continued barreling toward him. When she was within a few feet, he smiled, and said, "I see you got some shopping done."

That's when she descended on him with a screech, hair and bags flying in all directions, and whacked him on the side of the head with a shopping bag.

"You snake."

The fury that had consumed Callie in Smyth's office, when she'd found out her chivalrous husband had tricked her, bubbled through her veins once again. The discovery that Grandpa Ennis had left her oodles of money, and then spending a few of those oodles on clothes, had tempered the sting…until she saw the bum climb out of a cop car.

*A cop car?* He'd probably committed other criminal acts, in addition to scamming her for half of her ranch.

She'd nailed him on the side of the head with the first bag. *Time to renew the attack.* She swung a bag containing a shoe box in the general direction of his crotch, but he turned and the bag smacked his backside.

The same backside that had her fantasizing about making good on those wedding vows.

The realization that she still found the creep desirable zapped a raw nerve. She dropped her bags and charged him, but a pair of strong hands gripped her upper arms from behind. She scowled over her shoulder into a handsome face, split by a wide grin.

The cop found this amusing? She twisted in his grasp, stomping on his booted foot.

"Hey, are you trying to assault a sheriff?"

"Let her go, Rafe." Rod, a red welt streaking his face, stepped toward the cop.

A pinprick of guilt stabbed Callie. The corner of the shopping bag must have scratched his cheek.

The sheriff named Rafe released her and aimed a finger in her direction. "Do not renew your assault, or I'll haul your butt off to jail."

"Jail?" She pushed her hair out of her eyes. "That's a great idea. Arrest this man."

The sheriff's eyebrows disappeared beneath the rim of his white cowboy hat. She preferred Rod's black hat.

"Miss, you launched an unprovoked attack on him in the middle of the street. I witnessed it myself. Looked funny as hell, but that's beside the point."

"Go away, Rafe. I'll handle her." Rod began scooping up shopping bags from the sidewalk, shoveling frothy underwear into an overturned pink bag.

Callie's cheeks warmed to probably the same color

as the bag, while she pointed a wavering finger at Rod. "You handled me pretty well up to this point, didn't you, McClintock?"

The sheriff dragged his amused gaze away from the underwear and choked. "You know this woman, Rod?"

"She's my wife."

"What?" The sheriff backed up, stumbling against his squad car.

Callie swept her wagging finger toward the cop. "He married me under false pretenses to get his hands on my ranch. Can't you arrest him for that, or are you going to refuse to act because he's your buddy?"

Rod sighed and dug the heels of his hands into his eyes. "He's not my buddy. He's my brother."

Callie narrowed her eyes, shifting her gaze from one gorgeous brother to the other. Rod was a little taller, a little broader and a lot grumpier.

And a snake.

"Oh-ho. Perfect." She crossed her arms over her chest, tapping a sandaled toe.

"Perfect? This is not perfect." Rod jerked his chin toward his truck across the street. "Can we go somewhere and talk about this?"

After his initial shock, Rod's brother seemed to be enjoying himself immensely…at their expense. "Wait a minute. What's perfect?"

"Perfect that this lowdown, scheming husband of mine has a brother who's a cop. You're not going to arrest your own brother, are you?"

Rafe threw his head back and laughed, a sound so glorious and infectious it tugged at the corner of Callie's mouth. She valiantly fought the smile by twisting her lips into a sneer.

Give these McClintock brothers an inch and they'd have you weak at the knees and salivating.

"I can't arrest someone for marrying under false pretenses—unless he's already married." Rafe wiped his eyes. "Are you already married, Rod?"

"Shut up, Rafe."

Callie bit her lip, trying to keep the sneer in place. "Don't think I won't give up all this and get an annulment." She kicked one of the shopping bags. "I don't want you anywhere near *my* ranch."

"Miss...*Mrs.* McClintock." Rafe's sky blue eyes sparkled like the ocean on a summer day. Rod's eyes resembled a stormy jade sea. "I can assure you, my brother is not the type of guy to marry someone to get a ranch. He's not the type of guy to marry at all. And he already has a ranch."

"Yeah, one that marches right along next to mine."

That wiped the goofy grin off Rafe's face.

"Huh?"

Rod squeezed his turbulent green eyes shut for a second. "Rafe, this is Callie Price, Ennis Price's granddaughter, and the new owner of Price Is Right...and my wife."

Rafe worked his jaw before sputtering, "You own Price Is Right now? That's great!"

Rod's eyes were slits as he loomed over his younger brother, the menace in his stance slightly reduced by the colorful shopping bags clutched in his hands. "No. It's not."

"Dana is going to be really interested in meeting Callie." Rafe scratched his chin, shooting a glance at Rod.

"Not now, Rafe. I have some things to explain to my wife." He nudged her knee with a shopping bag. "Like how I didn't know she was Ennis Price's granddaughter until after the wedding."

Callie's foolish heart flip-flopped. "That's a good one. You probably followed me down to New Mexico. You probably paid off that valet parker to loan me his motorcycle. Maybe you even paid off those guys in the SUV on the highway so you could come to my rescue."

Rod shook his head. "That's crazy."

"Didn't I tell you insanity runs in my family?" She thrust out her chin.

"It does?" Rafe tripped off the curb on his way to the driver's side of his squad car.

"Don't you have a town to sheriff or something?" Rod eyed his brother with a dangerous glint.

"To be continued." Rafe got into his car, and with a wave of his hand pulled away from the curb.

Rod's gaze swept back to her, and for the first time Callie noticed he looked pretty ragged around the edges—unshaven, wrinkled shirt, wheat-colored hair sticking out in all directions…and a scratch on his cheek.

Callie clenched her jaw. The man had married her for her ranch. He'd tricked her. He'd lied to her.

God help her, she still wanted him.

He held up the bags, twined around his hands and wrists. "I'm going to load these up in my truck. They're cutting off my circulation."

With the pastel-hued shopping bags banging against his denim-clad legs, he stalked across the street. She followed. What choice did she have? He had all her new clothes in his possession.

After he dumped her purchases in the backseat of his truck, Rod grabbed her hand and pulled her across the sidewalk and into the park. Lacing his fingers through hers, he led the way down a cemented path toward a bench near a gurgling fountain.

Except for their breakneck pace and the scowl scribbled across Rod's face, they could be any newlywed couple enjoying an afternoon in the park.

Rod dropped onto the bench and pulled her down next to him. "I'm sorry."

His apology almost had her slipping off the edge of the bench. His entire demeanor had screamed anger and frustration…at her. Maybe she'd better listen to his side of the story before she renewed her attack.

"I knew who you were the minute you told me the name of your grandfather's ranch when we pulled out of Vegas." He held up his hands. "Not before. I tried to tell you then, but you were in no mood to talk. I planned to tell you last night and you fell asleep on me, or rather, on the couch."

Callie chewed her bottom lip. He had her there. She'd figured he was going to talk his way right out of a marriage he regretted, and she didn't want to hear it. "Are you trying to tell me that by pure chance we ran into each other on a highway in New Mexico?"

He slouched on the bench, tilting his head back to gaze at the sky—which looked like a perfect, blue Easter egg ringed by mountainous peaks.

"Chance or fate."

"You believe the stars destined our meeting? That our pairing was inevitable?"

He sent her a sideways glance full of liquid fire that ignited every nerve fiber in her body. Did he feel it then, too, this strong electric current between them?

He shrugged, dousing the fire. "I don't know. Call it coincidence."

She preferred the destiny thing.

"Why should I believe you?" Even though she wanted desperately to believe him.

She wanted to return to the time when she thought this chivalrous cowboy had come to her rescue just because. That the money she'd offered meant nothing to him. Now he stood to gain a lot more than money out of her.

"Because I don't lie." He draped his arm across the back of the bench, his fingers a whisper against her shoulder. "Old Ennis Price's ranch had been vacant so long, it didn't figure in my thoughts at all. I'd heard something about his will cutting out your father, Jonah Price, but I didn't know the details of his will. Nobody did."

Callie held her breath and hunched one shoulder to make contact with Rod's dangling fingers. They dabbled across her collarbone, and she closed her eyes, exhaling slowly through her nose. Did she dare believe him?

She couldn't allow this man's magnetism to cloud her judgment. Callie Price had never been anyone's fool. Well, except that Bobby had fooled her, and her father had fooled her on numerous occasions, and...*never mind*. She didn't plan on being anyone's fool from this point on.

Leaning forward, elbows on her knees, she said, "Actions speak louder than words. If you stick to our original agreement and make no claims on the land, I suppose I have no choice but to believe you."

His hand dropped to her curved back, and he ran a finger along her spine. "Okay, I'll take that. If I have to prove my innocence, I'll do it."

There was nothing innocent about the way she felt when Rod touched her. The pressure of his fingers tightened coils of desire in her belly. Any more time spent in his presence and *she'd* be the one having difficulty sticking to their agreement.

She combed shaky fingers through her hair. "Let's take

the first step then. Can you join me back at Doug Smyth's office to sign the deed to the ranch? His secretary has it ready for your signature, and she can notarize it, too. I already went to the bank and pulled out some cash, but I want the ranch in my name as soon as possible."

"Let's go." He pushed to his feet, running a hand over his face.

His disheveled appearance made him look sexier, like he'd just rolled out of bed, but she knew their antics over the past forty-eight hours had taken their toll on him, too. After they concluded their business with Smyth, they both needed some breakfast, and then Rod could return to his own ranch to shower, change and pick up where he left off before going to New Mexico and returning with a wife.

The thought of Rod vacating the ranch so soon after the wedding caused a lump to form in Callie's throat. Even though he still might be a snake.

They arrived at the law offices of Douglas Smyth and Sons, and Doug's secretary, Tanya, could barely keep her eyes in her sockets. "You could've bowled me over with a piece of lint when I found out you'd gotten married, Rod."

Rod grunted an unintelligible response and snatched a pen from the holder on the desk, while Tanya interrupted her boss's phone call to let him know the McClintocks had returned to sign the deed.

Tanya replaced the receiver of the phone. "You're one lucky girl, Callie. Do you mind if I call you Callie?"

Callie opened her mouth to say she didn't mind at all, but Tanya steamrolled over her response.

"There are plenty of women in Silverhill and beyond who thought they had a chance to tame this cowboy, only to fail."

Rod rolled his eyes at Callie, but she knew better. Her marriage to Rod had probably dashed the hopes of all the single ladies in Silverhill.

Tanya continued her chatter while Rod scrawled his signature on the deed to the ranch, and then in Tanya's notary book. After he gave her his thumbprint, he swiped his finger with the wipe she'd waved under his nose.

"Let's get some business done while we're here, and then breakfast." He tossed the wipe into the trash can and placed his hand on the small of Callie's back. She liked having his support, even if she still suspected his motives. Time would tell what he wanted out of her.

She already knew what she wanted out of him.

They had little time to talk in the next hour, as they both bought new cell phones and picked up a few supplies for the ranch.

WITH THEIR ERRANDS DONE, Rod pulled away from the curb and headed for the highway. Callie gripped the edge of her seat. "Are we having breakfast in Silverhill?"

Rod glanced at the clock on the dashboard. "More like lunch."

"But you'll know people there. What are you going to tell them about me?" The marriage scheme had sounded a lot easier when she believed they'd perpetuate it among strangers.

"The truth. I told you before. I don't lie."

Her gaze darted to his square jaw, clenched in determination. She'd never met anyone before who didn't lie. She came from a family of experts.

"Th-the whole truth?"

"I don't lie, but I'm not above omitting facts that belong between you and me."

He grinned, the first one she'd seen all morning, and suddenly the knot that had formed in her belly when she first discovered she'd married her neighbor, loosened.

"So tell me about Silverhill." Callie rolled her shoulders and settled into her seat. "Will I be accepted more readily, now that I'm married to one of Silverhill's favorite sons?"

Rod shot her a sidelong glance, and her face warmed. "I mean, for a little while anyway."

"I guess." He lifted his shoulders. "Why is it so important for you to be accepted by people you don't even know?"

She dropped her lashes, her nose tingling. "If I'm going to make Silverhill my home, I'd like to fit in. That's all."

"Well, I'm not the most popular McClintock in Silverhill. Hell, I'm not even the second most popular McClintock, so don't count on me to smooth any rough edges for you."

"Ah, smoothing rough edges reminds me. I'm going to make the first call on my new cell phone to my dad." She dug the new phone out of her new handbag and punched in his number. She held the phone away from her ear and said, "Voice mail."

She left her father a message, telling him the news about her marriage and assuring him she planned to make good on his debt to Bobby.

Snapping the phone shut, she said, "There. That should make Bobby feel a whole lot better."

"Not interested in Bobby feeling better. Just want him off your back."

Callie hid her smile as she shoved the phone back into her purse. She loved it when Rod said things like that.

SHE SPENT THE TWENTY-MINUTE drive back to Silverhill extracting bits of information out of Rod about her adopted town.

The ranching families, including the McClintocks, amassed their wealth through silver mining and decided to stay in the town that made them rich. Today the ski resort and tourism provided the jobs and money, although the residents didn't want another Aspen on their hands.

Rod pulled his truck up to the curb in front of a wood-sided restaurant with big windows looking out onto Silverhill's main street. The lace curtains at those windows twitched and Callie's nerves twitched along with them. Instead of acceptance, would she find hostility for snagging one of Silverhill's most eligible bachelors?

Shards of conversation from earlier in the day slanted through her mind, and she gripped the door handle as Rod eased to a stop. "Who's Dana?"

"Huh?" He switched off the engine and yanked the keys out of the ignition.

"When you and your brother were talking, he mentioned something about Dana being interested in meeting me. She's not a crazy ex-girlfriend or anything, is she? You assured me you were unattached."

"I am. I was. Dana is Rafe's wife. She grew up on the Ute reservation here and works for the FBI."

"FBI?" Callie swallowed. "Why would she be interested in me?"

Rod opened his door and said over his shoulder, "Because my sisters-in-law have been trying to set me up ever since they married my brothers."

She scrambled out of the truck before he could come around and open the door for her. She had to keep the focus of this marriage on the business aspect, not the wishful thinking part. That meant putting the brakes on

Rod's natural gallantry that led him to do crazy things like opening doors for her and carrying her bags…even the ones she'd used to smack him across his face.

They walked into the café and heads swiveled. At least there weren't that many heads in there to swivel. Callie gulped as she grabbed a seat facing the window, her back toward the prying eyes.

Rod exchanged greetings with a few old-timers and took the seat facing her. He snatched a couple of plastic-coated menus from the rack on the table and slid one to her. "Breakfast or lunch? I'm sure Sally will serve us either."

Callie dipped her head behind the menu as she felt heated interest buzzing behind her. "I think I'll have pancakes."

"Afternoon, Rod. What can I get you and your… friend?"

Callie glanced up into the smiling face of a woman with generous proportions. The light blue eyes above the smile brimmed with curiosity.

Rod took a deep breath. "This is Callie Price, Jonah Price's daughter, and the new owner of Price Is Right. She's also my wife."

The gasps behind her almost blew Callie over, and she gripped the edges of the menu. Rod sure liked to put it all out there.

Rod plowed on as if unaware he'd almost incited mass apoplexy in the other patrons. "Callie, this is Sally Jeffers, the owner of the Miner's Café."

Sally tucked her pencil behind her ear and extended a tattooed arm. "Nice to meet you, Callie. I never met your father, since he took off before I arrived. How'd you happen to hook up with Rod? I've never seen you in Silverhill before."

"Long story. Nobody's business. Let's just say I'm helping her out with the ranch."

Sally shrugged. "Okay, let's just say that. Welcome home, Callie. Now, what would you two newlyweds like?"

After they ordered, a chair scraped behind Callie and she held her breath. A shadow fell across the table. Rod glanced up and grimaced. "Hey, Grady."

The big man ignored Rod and squinted at Callie. "So you're Jonah Price's daughter."

"Yes." Callie gripped her hands in her lap, crushing her napkin. The man's heavy breathing made her nervous, and he smelled like garlic.

"You're married right and tight, and taking possession of Price Is Right?" He leaned his hands on the table, hunching his shoulders.

"Get off our table, Grady." Rod's brows collided over his nose.

Grady pushed off and smacked the table. "Just wanted an up close, personal look at the little gal who snatched that property from under my nose."

"What do you mean?" She hid her white knuckles beneath the table.

"If old Ennis's only heir didn't get married by the time she turned thirty-five, I'd take possession of that property and all the surrounding land." He shrugged. "I guess McClintock beat me to it."

Rod shoved out of his chair, knocking it to the ground. "I suggest you get the hell out of here, Grady."

Grady smirked and ambled out of the restaurant.

Callie exhaled. "So that's the associate who stood to inherit Grandpa Ennis's ranch. Why him?"

"Grady Pierce is the oldest son of the Pierce ranching family. Your grandmother was related to the Pierces. I guess your grandfather figured he'd keep the ranch in the family."

"And my grandfather thought that guy deserved it more than my father?" She stuck a finger in her mouth and gagged.

"Grady's a fine, upstanding citizen of Silverhill, with a growing family." Rod snorted. "He's also an ass."

When their food arrived, Rod dug into his ham and eggs. "So why do you think Bobby Jingo beat you to the ranch, broke in and left your veil? Do you think it's some kind of warning?"

"Not sure." Callie stabbed a whole blueberry from her pancake and popped it into her mouth. "I'm sure he didn't figure I'd marry the first man I saw after fleeing the wedding. Once Dad tells him I'm married, Bobby will expect me to make good on Dad's debt, which I will."

Rod sawed another piece of ham from the huge slab on his plate. "That would be the parking attendant."

"What?"

"The first man you saw—the valet parking attendant who loaned you his motorcycle. You'd be married to him now if you'd gotten hitched to the first man you saw."

She dabbed her lips with a napkin, hiding her smile. "Not at all. He was just a teenage boy, a rather grungy one at that."

"At least he'd be free of suspicion—I mean, not owning the ranch next to yours and all." Rod watched her over the rim of his coffee cup, humor glimmering around the edges of his dark green eyes. "Anyway, once you take some money out of the ranch and pay your father's debt, Bobby should leave you alone."

Callie gripped her bottom lip with her teeth. Should she tell him about her suspicions regarding Bobby? Rod might suspect her of playing him, just to keep him close.

What had Rod said about lying versus omitting certain facts? She could at least tell him she didn't have to take any money out of the ranch to pay off Bobby.

"I just hope he doesn't know about the rest of the money."

"The rest of what money?" Rod pushed away his plate and dug his elbows into the tabletop.

"Maybe I shouldn't be telling you this, but Grandpa Ennis left me a lot of assets and wealth beyond the ranch. I don't even have to borrow money against the ranch to pay Bobby."

"That doesn't surprise me. Old Ennis was tightfisted with a dollar and wouldn't give Jonah a dime. But it does worry me."

Callie's pulse ticked up a notch. "Why?"

"If Jingo knew about the other assets, he just lost more than a debt repayment. That's what bothered me about your story and Bobby's attempt to woo you back through kidnapping. Seems like a lot of trouble to go through just to get a couple hundred grand back—not that he wasn't getting a beautiful bride in the bargain."

"You don't have to tiptoe around my feelings, McClintock. I realize he wanted to marry me for the money and not my bubbling personality."

She pursed her lips as she drew patterns in the syrup with her fork. When she'd overheard Bobby talking about intercepting a shipment of drugs for Nick somebody, using the money from the ranch, it had puzzled her. Thanks to Mom, she knew a lot about obtaining multiple prescriptions for drugs, but she didn't know squat about drug dealing. But surely, a hundred thirty thousand wouldn't make much of a dent in the narcotics trade.

Her marriage to Rod had nipped that plan in the bud anyway. Bobby couldn't get his hands on her money now.

She'd pay off Dad's debt and be done with Bobby Jingo for good. He'd have to find another way to get into the drug trade.

Rod paid the bill again, but she didn't want to insist on paying now...in front of the whole town. She had a mental accounting of what she owed him, and planned to pay him back every penny.

They rumbled down the road toward Price Is Right while Callie studied her fingernails. "I suppose you want to go home to your own ranch. That's one advantage to being neighbors. We can stay married in name only and maintain separate residences."

Rod ran a hand over his mouth. "Yeah, that's a plus. I really need to shower and get a change of clothes. I feel like I've been through the hot cycle of a dryer."

Callie reached out and traced the scratch along Rod's jaw. "I'm sorry."

"I probably deserved that for not telling you my identity before you found out on your own."

A muscle in his jaw ticked beneath the pad of her fingertip, and she ran her thumb across his stubble. "You have an honest face, McClintock. You have me beginning to believe our encounter *was* pure chance."

"Keep your reservations, Callie. Trust should be earned, not given freely. Look what happened with Jingo." Rod stopped his truck in front of the secured gate and hopped out to unlatch it. He slid back into the truck and drove onto the driveway of the ranch house.

When he stopped the truck again, Callie shoved open her door. "My turn."

She slid the gate lock bolt back into place and returned to the truck. As they bounced along the unpaved driveway, Callie made a mental note to herself to spend some money getting it paved.

"Could you just help me with the bags? Then you can head back to your own place. I think I can have things under control here in a few days, and I'll get you your money."

"One thing at a time." Rod stomped on the parking brake and jumped from the truck.

Callie grabbed as many shopping bags as she could handle and then dug into her purse for the keys to the ranch, which Smyth had given her. She jingled them at Rod. "No more crawling through windows."

She unlocked the door and grabbed the bags she'd placed on the porch, nudging the door open with her hip. As her gaze darted around the living room, her jaw dropped.

Then she ran.

## Chapter Seven

Rod turned from the truck with bags in each hand. He took a step back when he saw Callie flying at him again. Had she changed her mind about trusting him?

Squealing, she threw herself against his chest and bounced off, since they both still clutched a ridiculous number of bags in their hands.

"What are you doing?"

She pointed toward the gaping door, a polka-dotted sack hanging from her wrist. "Someone broke in again, and this time he did more than leave a veil."

Rod dropped the bags and retrieved his gun from beneath his seat. He'd pulled out his weapon more times since meeting Callie than he had in the past ten years. "Do you want to wait here?"

She answered by sliding her fingers in his belt loop.

"Didn't think so."

Rod crept up the porch with Callie breathing heavily between his shoulder blades. He kicked the door wide and surveyed the damage. Someone had tossed the room—no other word for it. Papers littered the floor, cushions were scattered across the carpet and pictures on the wall tilted at odd angles.

Once again they searched the house and found nothing, but this time Rod wanted some answers. He righted a fallen kitchen chair and dropped into it. "What's Bobby Jingo after?"

Clutching her hands in front of her, Callie lifted her shoulders.

"Even if he doesn't know you're off the marriage market, what does he hope to gain by coming in here and trashing the place?" Rod leveled a finger at Callie, resolve forming a knot in his belly.

Callie's eyes widened. "M-maybe he's just trying to bully me into marrying him. Dad probably hasn't gotten my message yet, and Bobby still thinks he has a crack at me. Bobby probably knows I had more than just the ranch ripe for the picking, and he's willing to do anything necessary to get his hands on the cash."

Rod scanned the room between narrowed lids. "If he wanted to scare you, he'd pick a better method than this."

"Oh really?" Callie held trembling hands in front of her. "*This* is pretty scary."

Rod encircled her delicate wrists with his fingers. He'd prided himself on spotting deception a mile away. Had he allowed Callie to fool him with her fresh face and clear, blue eyes?

"Don't lie to me, Callie." Rising to his full height, Rod cinched his fingers tighter around her wrists and she flinched.

"I'm not lying." The pulse in her wrist fluttered in an unsteady beat. "I don't know what Bobby wants from me."

He loomed above her, his breath stirring the strands of her golden hair. "Why did you run out on him?"

She took a step back. "I told you. I couldn't go through with it once I found out it was a gambling debt and not a business deal. I didn't want to be married to a loan shark."

"You felt strongly enough about helping your father and making good on his investment to suggest the marriage in the first place. What changed your mind minutes before the ceremony? Did it really matter, that your father owed money to Bobby or what Bobby did for a living?"

A muscle twitched in his jaw. *And why was he asking her these questions just now?*

Her chest rose and fell rapidly, and then she slumped forward. "I discovered something about Bobby, other than the fact that he was a loan shark."

"What?" He growled the word through clenched teeth.

"Can you let go?" She flexed her fingers, and he dropped his hold on her. Taking a deep breath, she tossed her hair behind her shoulder and met his gaze. "About an hour before the ceremony, I went downstairs to Bobby's office to find a book of poetry."

"And what? You found out he preferred Wordsworth to Blake?"

She quirked an eyebrow at him. "I thought I was the smart aleck in this marriage?"

"Quit stalling."

"Actually, I brought the book with me from my father's place. I was planning to recite a few lines of poetry during our vows."

"How touching."

"Bobby had invited a bunch of people." She spread her arms out wide. "I wanted it to look realistic."

"What happened?"

"I found the book next to Bobby's computer. When I leaned over to get it, I noticed a financial spreadsheet with some staggering figures. Curiosity got the best of me, and

I started to scroll through the file to see if I could figure out what Bobby was tracking. I heard voices in the hall, and I panicked."

Rod sucked in his lower lip and tracked Callie as she picked up a cushion and settled it on the sofa before thumping it against her palm. Did she see something she wasn't supposed to see? His heart pounded against his ribcage, and he folded his arms across his chest to hide it.

He wasn't supposed to care this much.

A rosy pink tinged her cheeks as her lips twisted into a half smile. "I hid behind the drapes. Bobby came into the office with two of his associates. He always had men surrounding him wherever he went. Anyway, he started talking about a drug shipment, and how—with the money from the marriage—he was going to intercept it and put some other drug dealer out of business."

Rod blew out a breath, whistling in the process. "Did anyone see you? Did they know you were there?"

"No." She drew her brows together, wrinkling her nose. "I'm sure if he knew I was there, he would've yanked me out of my hiding place. But…"

"Go on." Rod bunched the material of his shirt in his fists.

"At one point Bobby stopped talking, and it sounded like he picked up a book and dropped it. I thought it might be my volume of poetry, but then he went on. I'm positive he didn't know I was hiding."

"Then he left the office, you grabbed your book and fled the scene."

"Sort of." She scooped some magazines off the floor and stacked them on the coffee table. "I escaped back to the room where I had been getting ready for the wedding, and warred with myself for over a half an hour before I decided to ditch the ceremony."

"So Bobby doesn't know why you ran out. He's just mad as all get out because he lost out on millions, money he planned to use to launch himself as a drug dealer." Rod sprang forward and started to help Callie pick up the room. "Let's face it, Callie. Your father must've told him about your grandfather's trust."

Her step faltered and she tripped on a rug in front of the fireplace. "I guess he did."

Rod grabbed her hand and smoothed a circle in her palm with his thumb. "He probably did it to assure Bobby you'd have enough cash to pay off his debt, not to hurt you."

She turned a bright blue gaze on him and snorted. "You wouldn't be so quick to make nicey-nice with his motives if you knew my father."

"Still doesn't explain what Bobby was looking for when he trashed this place."

"Maybe it wasn't Bobby. Maybe it was your garden variety thief assuming the place was empty."

"In Silverhill?" Even *she* didn't sound like she believed that. Would've been nice if she'd told him about the drugs before.

"You had a serial killer here last year. What's a little burglary?"

"I don't know, Callie. It doesn't add up."

"When my dad gets my message and passes it along to Bobby, this will all stop."

A muffled ring came from Callie's purse, hanging on the back of a chair. "That might be Dad now."

She flipped up the phone and flashed Rod a thumbs-up sign when she saw the display. "Hi, Dad. Did you get my message? Are you okay?"

Her father, his voice a little rough around the edges, answered, "I'm okay, and yeah I got your message. How did you manage to find someone to marry so quickly?"

Callie hunched over the counter separating the living room from the kitchen. "That's not important. I can get the money as early as tomorrow and give it to you. Then you can pay back Bobby yourself."

"Uh, about that."

"What?" She clutched the phone, and a pain stabbed her temple. "Did he hurt you?"

"No. I told you I'm okay. I'm more than okay. I'm far, far away from Bobby."

"Where are you?" Callie straightened her spine. Looked like Dad had taken care of himself, leaving her holding the bag...again.

"It's better you don't know, but that means *you'll* have to pay off Bobby for me. Can you do that?"

Anger thumped through Callie's veins. She'd been worried about Dad and he'd already made his escape. Okay, maybe she hadn't been as concerned about him as she should've been, but instead of the guilt she'd felt nibbling away at her conscience, she felt...justified.

"You mean you skipped out, leaving me to deal with Bobby by myself?"

Rod smacked down a roll of paper towel he'd just pulled from a bag and scowled in her direction. That scowl was enough to chill her blood, except Callie knew Rod intended it for her father and not her.

"I don't see it that way, Callie. Bobby's beef is with me, not you. It's better that I'm out of the picture."

"Better for whom?"

"Everyone. I'm going to give you Bobby's number. Call him and arrange for a drop."

"A drop?" She raised her brows at Rod and lifted her shoulders. His scowl deepened.

"Yeah, drop off the money. You don't want him coming to the ranch." He rattled off Bobby's cell phone number and Callie scribbled it on a receipt she'd pulled out of her purse.

"Wait, Dad. Did you know Grandpa had all these other assets?"

He sucked in a sharp breath. "I knew he probably had a little something. My father was a cheapskate. Never spent a dime he didn't have to. I figured he'd have a few bucks tucked away."

"It's more than a few bucks."

Rod made a hissing sound and drew his finger across his throat. Callie didn't figure it mattered now. The money was hers fair and square and legal, but she pursed her lips.

"You don't have to worry about me, Callie. I appreciate your paying off my debt, and that's all I'll ask of you. Me? I'm going to hit the road. I have your stuff, and I'll send it to you at the ranch."

And with that he ended the call.

Callie snapped her phone shut and tapped it against her chin. "Sounds like he didn't realize how much money Grandpa Ennis left in the trust—and he's definitely not interested in getting his hands on it."

Crossing his arms, Rod leaned his hip against the counter. "And you believe him? Callie, he just left you alone to clean up his mess with some two-bit loan shark and wannabe drug dealer. Do you trust anything out of the man's mouth?"

Did she? She believed him when he told her his deal with Bobby was a failed investment. She believed him when she assured her that he'd be there for her college graduation. She believed him when he promised to take her back to Colorado to visit her grandparents.

And he'd disappointed her every time.

How many times would she keep banging her head against the wall and hope for a different result, other than pain and heartache? It just hurt so damned much to accept that your father didn't give a rat's behind about you.

She dropped her lashes over the tears threatening to pool in her eyes. Then she shrugged and flashed Rod a phony grin. "My father's a character."

Rod took two steps toward her and ran a fingertip from her earlobe to her jaw. "I misspoke. He didn't leave you all alone to deal with this. You have me."

"No." She shook her head so hard, her hair whipped back and forth. "You've done your part to help me out. You don't need to be involved in my problems anymore."

He cupped her face in his hands. "You're wrong. We're married, at least on paper, and I take my responsibilities very seriously."

As she looked up into his eyes, a hot tear escaped and ran toward her ear. Rod caught it with his thumb. He brushed his lips across hers in a whisper of a kiss. "Don't worry. I'll take care of Bobby Jingo *and* your father, if he tries something."

Callie sniffled and managed a watery smile, a real one this time. She'd never had someone on her side before. But who was she kidding? She'd entered into a sham marriage, and when it ended, she'd better be prepared instead of floating along in dreamland.

She ducked to the side and held up her phone. "I'm going to call Bobby right now and take care of this."

"Put him on speaker, and for one time only, follow your father's advice. Set up a drop location. You don't want him here at the ranch."

She smoothed the crumpled receipt on the counter and punched in Bobby's number with her heart pounding. He answered immediately.

"Bobby, this is Callie...Price." He didn't need to know the identity of her new husband.

"Quite a stunt you pulled. Not much of a devoted daughter, are you?"

"I have your money."

"You mean you actually plan to make good on Jonah's debt?"

"Sure I do. Why wouldn't I? Even if you're a loan shark and not the injured party in a business deal, my father still owes you the money, and I'm going to pay it back for him."

"That's why you ran?"

"That's not enough? You're in a dirty business and I don't trust you." Callie held her breath. Bobby had to believe she knew nothing more about his dirty business or his plans for making it dirtier.

Bobby let out a long breath, as if he'd been holding it like her. "I'm staying in a bed-and-breakfast in Silverhill, by the river. Do you know where it is?"

*God, he had been lurking in Silverhill.* Callie glanced at Rod and he nodded. "Yeah, what time?"

"The sooner I get my money the better. How about noon? That'll give you time to get it from the bank."

"Okay, but I'm bringing my husband, so don't try anything funny."

"Wouldn't dream of it. One more thing, Callie. Where's your father?"

Callie's pulse ticked up a notch. "I don't know. Why? I have the money, not him."

"Just wondered where he ran off to after you ditched the wedding."

"I don't know. He didn't tell me, which isn't unusual."

They ended the call and Callie turned to Rod. "So what do you think?"

"Sounds like he wants his money. Sounds like he wants your father, too. What would Bobby want with Jonah, once you pay his debt? Your father must have escaped from Bobby after that phone call to you."

"My father's good at wheedling his way out of trouble. Maybe he convinced Bobby he could get me to go through with the wedding."

"I don't like it, Callie. I'm going to the bank with you tomorrow, and I'll be there when you meet Bobby."

"I'm counting on it. Now you probably want to get home. I—I'll call you tomorrow morning."

Rod's brows disappeared beneath a lock of hair. "I'm not leaving you until that debt is paid and Bobby is out of Silverhill, if I have to personally escort him myself."

"Rod, you haven't been home yet. At least I had a quick shower this morning and changed my clothes when I went shopping. I'll bet you didn't even have that luxury."

"That bad, huh?" He grinned as he pulled his shirt away from his body.

Actually, she loved his scent, gritty and totally male.

"Not bad at all, considering. But I insist you go home."

He grabbed her hand. "Only if you come with me. It'll give me a chance to pick up some materials to repair that window—and a few other things around here."

"You don't…"

"Stop." Rod sliced his other hand through the air. "We're married. Let's just pretend for a few days."

The butterflies in Callie's stomach went crazy. She'd

love to play make-believe with Rod, but she wouldn't have to playact in the bedroom.

Her attraction to her new husband was for real.

WARM WATER STREAMED DOWN Rod's back as he soaped up his chest and shoulders. He didn't like the idea of Callie handing over a bundle of cash to a lowlife like Bobby Jingo.

Bobby's current residency in Silverhill didn't surprise Rod. He'd broken into the ranch not once but twice. He'd come through the same window the second time, busting through the plywood covering the window. What did he want from Callie?

He turned to face the spray of water, running his hands through his wet hair. Bobby hadn't realized Callie had gotten married until Jonah called him this afternoon. Maybe that's why he ransacked the ranch. If Bobby couldn't collect on his debt, he'd take anything he could get.

Rod massaged the back of his neck. Then why didn't Bobby take anything? Of course, Callie didn't know if there had been any jewelry or money on the premises, or anything else of value to steal, but this crime looked like a search, not a theft.

They'd find out tomorrow when they turned the money over to Bobby. Rod had every intention of being there to protect Callie if things got ugly.

Rod finished his shower, shaved and put on some clean clothes. As he jogged downstairs, the unmistakable smell of barbecue greeted him.

Callie looked right at home making a salad in the kitchen. His breath hitched. This sure looked real for being make-believe.

"You didn't have to make dinner."

"I figured I owed you, after you fixed the window, shored up the sagging porch and cleared those weeds from the front. Besides, I've been practicing my culinary skills for the past year."

He sluiced his wet hair back from his face. "Why practice cooking? Were you planning to get married to grab that inheritance?"

She shook her head and then popped a cherry tomato from the garden into her mouth and rolled her eyes upward. "Besides, making dinner is easy when you have all those amazing veggies in the garden, a couple of steaks in the freezer and that gleaming gas barbecue on the patio. Doesn't look like it gets much use."

"My dad likes to barbecue. I haven't used it much since he and my stepmother moved out of the ranch."

"When they moved out they left the ranch to you?"

"Mostly. I was already on the title of the ranch and most of the property, but my father is turning over several hundred acres to a long-lost half brother of mine."

Her knife paused above a green pepper. "You have a long-lost half brother?"

"He hasn't responded to my father yet, so I don't know what's going to happen next. I've written off that parcel of land."

Tucking her tongue in the corner of her lip, Callie sliced into the pepper. "Now you have *my* ranch."

Rod braced his hands on the counter and leaned forward. "Are we back to that again? You still have doubts."

"You're the one who told me not to trust too quickly." She waved the knife in the air, and he eyed it uneasily.

"That's right. I'll prove I want nothing out of you." The lie stuck in Rod's throat. He wanted plenty out of this feisty little blonde, and it had nothing to do with land.

ROD ENJOYED THE MEAL, washing down the last bite of the peppery steak with a gulp of cold beer. The conversation had been even better than the food.

He collected their dishes and stacked them in the sink. "With your background, I didn't have you pegged as the domestic type. You're a good cook."

"Living with my mom, we ate a lot of take-out and frozen food. Not the healthiest diet. So I figured it was time to start cooking." She joined him at the sink. "You rinse. I'll stick them in the dishwasher."

They finished cleaning up, side-by-side, and then Rod invited her to the porch swing. They'd been on a roller coaster these past few days, and the knots in his neck were just starting to unwind.

Callie sank down next to him, gripping the heavy chain that suspended the swing from the beams above the porch. "Just for a few minutes. I should get back to the ranch."

Rod pushed off, setting the swing in motion. "You're staying here tonight."

"What?" She thumped against the back of the swing, her feet flying in the air.

"Bobby's in town. He broke into your place twice. We don't know what he wants." *And I don't want you out of my sight for one minute.*

"I don't want to disrupt your life any further, Rod."

He tipped back his head and laughed. He'd gone down to New Mexico to look at some horses and wound up with a wife, who happened to live next door, and some shady loan shark on his tail. How could one overnight guest cause any more turmoil?

Callie giggled. "I guess it's a little late to be worrying about that now, isn't it?"

"You don't even need to go home. I have extra toothbrushes and spare rooms with clean sheets. My housekeeper, Greta, keeps the house as if she expects a passel of McClintocks to descend at any second."

"Will they?" Callie tucked her hands beneath her thighs and peered into the darkness at the edge of the driveway.

"Don't worry. No chance of that."

"I wasn't worried. I think it might be kind of interesting to have a house full of people."

"*Interesting* is a good word."

THEY SPENT THE NEXT FEW HOURS on the porch swing, talking. Callie still hedged around, as if guarding portions of her life she didn't want him to enter. If she planned to stay on at Price Is Right, they'd have plenty of time to get to know each other better.

No need to rush anything.

Rod stood up and stretched. "Are you ready to turn in? Tomorrow's going to be another busy day for you."

She uncurled her legs and extended them in front of her, pointing her toes. "Yeah, I can't wait to get the first part over. Paying off Bobby. Do you mind if I take a shower?"

"Nope. I'll get you a towel and show you the room. There's a bathroom connected to this particular guest bedroom."

She followed him upstairs, her breath coming in short spurts. She didn't appear to be out of shape. Glancing over his shoulder, he asked, "You okay?"

"I'm fine." She grasped the banister, her blue eyes wide.

He continued to the landing and threw open a door in the hallway. "The bed is already made, and the bathroom is through that door."

"Thanks. I'll head home tomorrow morning and then

out to the bank in Durango. I'll meet you back at the ranch."

"You can't get rid of me that easily, Callie. You don't even have a car, and I'm not going to let you carry around that kind of cash by yourself. You're stuck with me until we see Bobby."

"Okay." She placed her hand on his forearm and he felt branded by her cool fingers. "I really appreciate your support, Rod. You'll be off the hook soon."

"Stop worrying about me. You probably spent all your time as a kid worrying about your parents. Let it go."

He brushed his fingers across her cheek, and she closed her eyes. Pinching her chin, he said, "Get some rest."

She shut the door and he wandered off to his own bedroom, wondering if he *wanted* to be off the hook.

He pulled off his T-shirt and tossed it into the hamper. Then he brushed his teeth and splashed some water on his face. He turned on the light over his bed, grabbed his biography of Winston Churchill and punched his pillows against the headboard.

He started unbuttoning his jeans when he heard the shower turn off. Callie probably needed something to wear to bed…considering she wasn't going to wear him. Not tonight anyway.

He buttoned his fly and pulled one of his T-shirts off a hanger in the closet. He crept down the hall toward her bedroom door and knocked. When she didn't answer, he eased the door open and stepped inside the room.

The bathroom door was open a crack and the fan whirred behind it, sending tendrils of lilac steam into the bedroom. Rod tossed the T-shirt onto the bed and turned to leave.

Callie squealed and he spun around. She was tucking

the corner of a towel into the edge under her arm, and her long ponytail slid over one shoulder.

"Sorry." Rod backed up a few steps and gestured toward the T-shirt draped over the foot of the bed. "Thought you might want something to wear to bed. I knocked."

She folded her arms across her chest, eyes bright above pink cheeks. "I didn't hear. Thanks for the T-shirt."

"Sure." He stumbled out of the room and cursed himself until he yanked off his jeans and flung himself onto his own bed.

*Smooth, McClintock.*

He'd behaved like an awkward teenager. Did Callie want him to whip off that towel and take her in his arms?

He snorted and cracked open his book. Didn't look like she shared his fantasies. Not one bit.

THE FOLLOWING MORNING, Callie folded Rod's T-shirt neatly and laid it on the pillow. Last night she'd enjoyed snuggling in something that had been right next to his body. Not that she got much sleep.

Why did she scream when she saw him in the room? She should've come up with some sultry line to lure him into bed instead of chasing him away.

She poked her head into the hallway. She didn't even know which bedroom he occupied. And if she did? She didn't have the guts to make a move on her own husband.

The smell of coffee drew her downstairs like a magnet, and she discovered Rod hunched over a newspaper at the kitchen table. He looked up, a lock of sandy hair falling over one eye. "Sleep okay?"

She lied through her forced smile. "Yes, I did. You?"

"Uh-huh." He snapped the newspaper. "Coffee?"

"Sure." She stumbled into the kitchen. They were acting like a couple who'd just had a one-night stand, instead of newlyweds who hadn't so much as kissed. *Well, not exactly.* Technically, their lips had met a few times. Rod's had felt smooth and warm and delicious.

"Callie?"

"Huh?"

Rod raised his brows, pointing at the coffeepot she held suspended over her cup. "Are you going to pour it, or what?"

She splashed some coffee in the cup and spun toward the refrigerator for some milk. She'd better snap out of these daydreams about her new husband. He still had to prove himself, and she didn't plan on giving him a pass.

"I'm assuming the Bank of Colorado in Durango opens at nine. I'll go home to change clothes, and then you can pick me up. I'll take care of some more business while we're in Durango, and then we can come back to Silverhill to meet Bobby."

"Sounds good. I'll wait for you while you change."

Looked like she had a bodyguard for the duration, or at least until she turned the money over to Bobby.

Marriage had its benefits.

A FEW HOURS LATER, after she'd done a few errands in Durango and withdrew the money her dad owed Bobby, she and Rod headed back to the ranch.

Callie put her groceries away while Rod transferred the cash from the satchel they'd taken to the bank to two paper bags. "Bobby will probably want to count the money. As soon as he's satisfied, we'll make sure he leaves town."

"Then…" Callie folded and creased the shopping bags, dipping her head while her hair shielded her face.

"Then I can get back to the business of running my

ranch, and you can decide if you really want to stay in Silverhill."

"Oh, I plan to stay here. I think it would be a great place for...me." *Not to mention Jesse.*

"First things first. Let's get this scumbag Bobby out of your life."

Rod loaded the bags of cash in the backseat of his truck, and Callie hopped in beside him. She rubbed her palms on the thighs of her shorts and took a deep breath. She hadn't faced Bobby since the night before the wedding ceremony that wasn't, before she found out his true ambitions.

Rod pulled the truck across the street from a neat Victorian bed-and-breakfast, with a gurgling creek running along the side of the property.

Callie inhaled the fresh air, the water creating a soothing murmur in the background. "Bobby has good taste."

Rod laughed. "I don't think Gracie Malone, the owner of this B and B, would've accepted his reservation, had she known about his past."

"Bobby puts on a good act. He fooled me—for a while."

"I'm surprised he's not meeting us out front. Is that his car?" Rod pointed to a black Escalade.

"That's one of them, anyway."

Rod's boots crunched the gravel as he strode toward the front of the B and B, the paper sacks swinging from his hands as if they contained bananas instead of over a hundred thousand dollars.

He pushed open the door, the stained glass set in an archway at the top catching the afternoon light and spilling it on the gleaming hardwood floor. He called out, "Gracie?"

A woman scurried from the back, clutching a dish towel. "Hello, Rod."

"We're looking for one of your guests, Bobby Jingo."

Gracie's beady, dark eyes brightened and Callie swallowed. Nosey people. One of the joys of small-town life.

"Do you know that nice young man?" As Gracie spoke to Rod, her gaze darted toward Callie.

"We have a little business with him." Rod pressed the bags against his legs.

"I heard the front door about fifteen minutes ago, so he may have gone out. Most of my other guests left for excursions this morning." She tucked a strand of graying hair back into her bun. "Are you going to introduce me to your wife, Rod?"

Callie shot a glance at Rod. News traveled fast. Another feature of small-town life.

"Gracie, this is Callie. Callie, Gracie Malone."

As they shook hands, Gracie devoured Callie with her gaze. "Imagine that. You married Ennis's granddaughter. I remember you the few times you came to visit, Callie. Your mother didn't much like Silverhill—not enough excitement for her, I guess. Didn't she have a rather tragic ending?"

Callie clenched her fists. She gathered a deep breath, getting ready to put this rude woman in her place, but Rod grabbed her hand.

"You can get to know Callie better later, Gracie. We have to find Bobby."

Rod tugged Callie out of the room, as its pleasant pots of potpourri began to suffocate her. They landed outside and Callie gulped in several breaths of fresh air. "That woman."

"She's the town gossip. Don't worry about Gracie." He cocked his head at her. "Something you're going to have to get used to if you plan to stay in Silverhill."

Why did it always seem like Rod was trying to drive

her away? "Whatever. Let's unload this cash and get out of here. Where do you think he went?"

"I have no idea. Maybe a walk along the riverbank." He turned a corner around the main house, striding toward a smaller house set among the trees and closer to the creek.

A shiver rippled up Callie's back and she slipped her hand around Rod's arm. "This place is kind of creepy."

"Really? You feel it? A woman was murdered here just over a year ago."

"Did they catch her killer?" She cinched his wrist with her other hand.

"Yeah."

The menacing air didn't seem to deter Rod as he clumped down to the water's edge, clutching the handles of the paper bags while Callie clutched him.

He yelled, "Bobby."

Callie peered around Rod's shoulder, along the rocky banks of the creek. "I don't see him. Let's go."

Rod held up his hand. "Wait. Did you hear that?"

She tilted her head and held her breath. Over the splashing water, she heard a few twigs snap. Nothing out of the ordinary for the great outdoors.

"I don't hear anything."

He put his finger to his lips and pressed the bags of cash into her hands. A trail of rocks crossed the creek to the other bank, and Rod put a tentative foot on the first one.

"I'm over here." Bobby emerged from the bushes on the other side of the creek, slicking his dark hair off his forehead. He pointed to Callie. "If that's the money, you two can bring it over here. I'll count it and be on my way."

Callie nudged in behind Rod and held a bag out to him. "Let's go."

"Wait." Rod put a hand on her waist. "We're on this side, Jingo, along with your car. You come over here and you'll get your money."

"I thought it would be more private over here. Gracie has guests coming and going, and they like to take that path along the creek and cross the bridge at the end, where it expands."

"We'll stay here." Rod widened his stance.

Bobby glanced over his shoulder, licking his lips.

"Get down!" Rod pushed Callie to the ground. Before she toppled over, she saw Bobby drop to his knees and then fall face forward into the creek.

# Chapter Eight

The hand gripping the weapon materialized from the trees again, and Rod fell on top of Callie, shielding her body. A spitting sound came from the trees and something whizzed above his head.

The shooter had switched his target from Bobby to them. Rod wrapped his arms around Callie and rolled behind a boulder. He held her head against his thundering heart.

Rod dug his cell phone out of his pocket and punched in 911. He got Deputy Brice Kellogg at the Silverhill Sheriff's station. "It's Rod. There's been a shooting on Gracie Malone's property, and the shooter just fired at us."

Callie gasped into his chest and he stroked her hair. Why hadn't he brought his gun? He'd had a bad feeling about this meeting from the get-go.

He ended the emergency call and peeked around the rock. Bobby's body sprawled half into the creek, his legs stretched out behind him. If the bullet hadn't killed him, the water had finished the job.

Callie shifted beneath him and whispered, "Did you see who shot him?"

He shook his head and placed a hand over her mouth. He didn't know if the killer had seen them tumble behind this rock or not, but he didn't want to take any chances.

From his position, he could see anyone crossing the creek bed, and it would take them several minutes to get to the bridge or come around the other side.

He'd keep Callie safe here until the cops arrived.

A siren blared in the distance and Rod hugged Callie tighter. "You're okay."

Two squad cars squealed to a halt in front of the bed-and-breakfast. Kellogg hopped out of one and Rafe jumped from the other.

Rod rose from his cramped position and waved to them. "Over here." He kept a hand on top of Callie's head, to keep her behind the rock.

Both deputies jogged along the side of the B and B, guns drawn. Gracie trailed after them until Rafe turned and said something to her and she retreated.

"What's going on here, Rod? Are you okay?"

"We're fine, but he's not doing so well." Rod jerked his thumb toward Bobby's body.

Rafe cursed and picked his way across the creek bed to Bobby's prone form. Squatting down, he pulled a pair of gloves out of his back pocket and slipped them on his hands. He placed two fingers on Bobby's neck.

"He's dead."

Callie choked as she wrapped her arms around Rod's left boot. Rod ran his fingers through her sun-warmed hair. "I think it's okay now."

She slid up his body, clinging to his arm. "Why would someone kill Bobby?"

"I can think of several reasons." He brushed some dirt and pebbles from her smooth thigh. "Let's find out."

He pulled her from their protective rock, still keeping her behind him. "I saw a gun sticking out of those trees. Someone must've been hiding back there."

Rafe's radio crackled as he called in an ambulance. Brice crept toward the trees bordering the creek, his weapon ready.

"You knew him?" Rafe's eyes narrowed as he zeroed in on the paper bags Rod had left by the boulder.

"Name's Bobby Jingo. We were meeting him to pay off a debt for Callie's father."

Rafe groaned and stalked toward the bags, peering inside. "Do you have your gun?"

"Do you think I shot him?" Rod followed him and then crossed his arms over his chest. "If I'd had my gun, that SOB in the trees would be joining Bobby in the ambulance right about now."

Rafe twisted his head around. "Find anything, Brice?"

"Just a few recently snapped twigs. Looks like the shooter fled the scene in a hurry."

Turning back to Rod, Rafe said, "Give it to me from the beginning."

From the beginning? *Not a chance, little brother.*

Callie pinched Rod's forearm…hard. Did she really think he'd spill the whole story?

Rod told Rafe everything he saw and heard from the moment he and Callie spotted Bobby across the river. Then he tersely explained how Jonah Price called Callie and asked her to meet Bobby to pay off a gambling debt for him.

"Why didn't he pay it himself?" Rafe scribbled the last of Rod's details in his notebook.

"He didn't have the money." Callie kicked one of the cash-filled bags on the ground. "He asked me to pay the debt…literally and every other way."

Rafe tapped his pen against the notebook. "Kind of lucky you just came into the money to pay that debt."

"Lucky's my middle name." She shoved her hands in the pockets of her shorts, hunching her shoulders.

Rafe's gaze traveled from Callie's face to Rod's. "Had you met Mr. Jingo before today, Ms.—Mrs.—Callie? Or should I just call you 'Lucky'?"

"Callie's good. After all, we're family." She nudged Rafe's arm with her elbow. "I saw Bobby around a few times while I was visiting my dad in New Mexico."

"Did you realize he was a loan shark, your father's bookie?"

"I didn't figure him for a Boy Scout, but I didn't inquire too closely. Probably got whacked by a client, don't you think?"

"Maybe. Where's your father?"

"I don't know. That's why I'm here and he's not."

The wail of the ambulance siren cut through the quiet countryside, and Rod blew out a long, steady breath. Although Callie remained as smooth as one of those pebbles in the creek under Rafe's questioning, Rod welcomed the distraction of the ambulance.

Rafe slid his notebook in his pocket. "I'm going to question Gracie to see if Jingo had any visitors during his brief stay—I mean, other than you two. Don't take any sudden trips."

"You know where I live." Rod hoisted the bags in his arms.

"And where would that be? At your wife's ranch or your own?"

Rod raised the bags higher to obscure his face. "We're staying at my place until we do a few more repairs on Price Is Right. Then…we'll figure it out."

"I'm sure you will." Rafe called Brice over, and the two of them conferred with the EMT before trudging across the property to question Gracie.

Callie tugged at his sleeve. "I guess he suspects something fishy, huh?"

"Guess so." He watched the EMTs load Bobby's body into the back of the ambulance. "Did Bobby have any enemies in New Mexico?"

"Probably. He always had big, burly guys around him. I figured those men must be bodyguards or something. You saw them—the two who came after me."

Rod tugged on his ear. "I wonder why he came alone this time. Did you get the impression he knew he had company in the trees behind him?"

"He looked nervous." She scrunched up her face. "But maybe he just heard a noise. The killer used a silencer, huh? That's why we didn't hear a gunshot."

"Yep. A professional. Are you thinking what I'm thinking? Maybe that drug dealer got wise to Bobby and decided to stop him before he could make a move." It's a good thing Callie overhead that conversation, or, as Bobby's wife, she might have been in the path of a vindictive drug dealer.

"I thought about that." Her gaze wandered over the trees on the other side of the creek. "But why did the killer turn the gun on us?"

"Getting rid of witnesses."

"I suppose you're right." She hugged herself and gave an exaggerated shiver. "If I had gone through with the marriage to Bobby, I might be in a lot of danger right now."

"That occurred to me, too. As it is…" He trailed off. *As it is, she still might be in danger.* "Let's get this money back in the bank."

"Does this mean my father doesn't owe the money on his debt anymore?"

"Depends on whether or not Bobby left his IOUs to

anyone. That could be another motive for the murder. Someone owed Bobby too much money to pay back."

Callie dropped her lashes over her eyes. "Whatever the motive, Bobby's not my problem anymore."

Rod handed her one of the paper bags as he drew his brows over his nose. "No, he's not."

AFTER THEY RETURNED TO the bank to redeposit the money, Callie continued shopping for supplies and groceries. Rod helped out with a few more chores around the ranch, until she sent him home. The Price Is Right ranch could keep Rod occupied for months, but Callie needed to start distancing herself from his solid shoulder.

Taking the first step in this process, she purchased new linens and staked out the master bedroom as her own. She couldn't bear to sleep another night under Rod's roof, with Rod inhabiting another bed. He'd been so darned helpful all day, not even complaining once that she'd involved him with an unsavory character like Bobby, who'd wound up murdered.

Her feelings for Rod scared her. When he touched her or smiled at her with that crooked grin, she'd float along in a rainbow-hued bubble, setting herself up for the big fall. Once he discovered her emptiness, he'd flee faster than a jackrabbit in a forest fire.

She'd been in relationships before, but all the men she dated had been unavailable in one way or another. She gravitated toward that type of man. When the end came, she didn't care. They'd both move on to other superficial couplings.

She didn't need her unworthiness validated by someone of substance. Someone like Rod.

Dropping into a chair by the window, she kicked her

feet up on the ottoman and cracked open a can of diet soda. She had a few phone calls to make.

Hearing Jesse's voice always plucked her out of a self-pitying mood. She called the L.A. County Department of Child and Family Services to get the number of his current foster family, and to update them on her status and renew her petition for adoption.

Callie had met Jesse when she'd volunteered to teach art classes at a summer camp for kids in the system. His big, brown eyes had stolen her heart, and when she found out his dad had died of a drug overdose and his mom had dropped her five-month-old infant in a trash bin, it sealed the deal.

The county accepted her application as a foster parent and she'd had Jesse for eight glorious months. Just when she'd decided to adopt him, she lost her studio and her home to the fire. DCFS had put her petition for adoption on hold, but agreed to reconsider once she got her life back together.

Well, she was in the process of doing that now. Maybe she had a chance to make a home for Jesse.

She called Jesse's foster family, and his foster mother, Gail Bishop, answered the phone. Gail had a big home and a bigger heart. She'd taken in several kids over the past twenty years, and put in a good word for Callie with DCFS, telling the agency that Jesse belonged with Callie.

"Gail, it's Callie Price. Can I speak to Jesse?"

"Callie, are you still in New Mexico? Jesse sure misses you, but he's at the pool with my husband and some of the older kids."

Disappointment punched Callie in the gut. "I'm in Colorado now. I have a home and a…a husband."

"That's wonderful, dear. Congratulations. I don't see how the county can refuse you now. Jesse needs a nice, stable environment."

Callie could give him that, even without Rod. But the county didn't need to know her marriage was a two-year deal.

"I already gave DCFS my new information and requested a visit with Jesse out here, and a reopening of my adoption petition."

"I hope it all works out. We'll keep him safe until he can join you. Another foster family inquired about Jesse a few months ago, but we didn't want to give him up."

"Another family?" Callie gripped the phone. "Really?"

"Yes, but apparently they were new to the system and didn't qualify. Don't worry. Jesse's doing fine, although he's been acting out a little. I show him your picture every day, and he makes up stories about what you're doing."

Callie smiled and wiped a tear from her cheek. Even a kid with Jesse's amazing imagination couldn't come up with the stuff she'd been living with the past week.

"I appreciate it, Gail. Can you please call me when he gets back from the pool?"

They ended the call and Callie retrieved a tissue from the bathroom and blew her nose. She didn't want Jesse to feel abandoned.

She knew all too well how that felt.

Picking up her cell phone, she steeled herself for a less pleasant call. She punched in her father's number and chewed the inside of her cheek while his phone rang.

The call connected, but Callie heard only breathing, no voice. "Dad?"

"Callie?"

"Yeah. Where are you?"

"On the road. I hope you're calling to tell me you paid off Bobby without any problems."

She twisted the pop-top off her soda and dropped it in the can. "I wouldn't exactly say that."

Dad drew in a sharp breath. "What happened?"

"Bobby's dead."

"What?" Dad choked and cursed.

"My husband and I went to meet him at a bed-and-breakfast here in Silverhill, and somebody shot him—right in front of us."

"Are you okay?"

"Other than witnessing the murder of a guy I'd almost married, sure."

"It's not like Bobby was the love of your life or anything. Who shot him?"

"You tell me."

"Why would I know?"

"I think you know a lot more about Bobby and his business than you're letting on."

"Are you telling me that you didn't see his killer?"

"That's right."

He let out a long breath. "That's a good thing. But stand by. Someone else may be knocking on your door to collect that debt."

"Why *my* door?" She punched the cushion of the chair. "Why don't they contact *you?*"

"I'm out of it, Callie. Just turn over the money when they come calling, and you can honestly tell them you don't know my whereabouts."

"Wait a minute. If I turn over the money, why would they care about you?" The back of her neck tingled when she recalled Bobby asking about Dad.

"You don't know where I am. You didn't have any contact with me after you fled the wedding. Stick to that story, and you'll be okay."

The tingle raced down her spine. "What story? That's *the truth*. What's going on, Dad? What did you get yourself into?"

He laughed, a sharp sound that made her wince. "It's all good, Callie. You enjoy your married life and that ranch, and all that money my father left you. You deserve it. God dealt you a helluva hand when you wound up with Diane and me as parents."

That's the closest her father had ever come to acknowledging his inadequate parenting skills. Before Callie could recover from her shock and pick up her jaw from the floor, her father ended the call.

She recognized Dad's tap dancing skills. He knew more than he was telling, but she'd look out for Bobby's replacement and pay him off, too.

She checked the time on her cell phone and dropped it back onto the coffee table. Rod had mentioned something about dinner when he left, but she'd insist on staying at her own place tonight.

A sharp rap on the front door propelled her from the chair, and she peeked out the window. A woman with shoulder-length dark hair stood on the porch, tapping the toe of her red boot.

A neighbor being friendly maybe? Callie opened the door and smiled.

The woman's dark eyes brightened. "Hi. I'm so sorry to disturb you, but I ran out of gas on my way into Silverhill, and my cell phone is dead. Can I borrow your phone or bother you for a lift into town?"

"I don't have a car, but you're welcome to use my cell." Callie left the door open and turned to retrieve her phone. "Do you live in Silverhill?"

Callie grabbed her cell and spun around, almost colliding with the woman who had followed her inside. "Sorry."

"No, I'm sorry. I still feel kind of clumsy in these boots." She glanced down at the pointy-toed red cowboy boots and grimaced.

"Does that mean you're not from around here?" Callie extended her phone to the woman, who pinched it between elegant fingers with long, painted nails.

The woman laughed. "Is it that apparent? I'm house hunting for a winter home. I want something close to a ski resort, but I've had my fill of Aspen and even Jackson Hole. Looking for something a little quieter, and a friend mentioned Silverhill. I also heard the prices were better during the summer."

"I haven't been here that long myself, but it seems like a nice town."

The woman held out her hand. "I'm Amber Lewis."

"Callie Price, I mean McClintock."

Amber's dark sculpted brows shot up. "Can't remember your own last name?"

"I got married recently." Callie wiggled her ring finger, Rod's cheap ring catching the sunlight from the window. "Still getting used to it."

"I know what you mean."

"Are you here with your husband?" Callie peeked out the front door. Opening her home to a single woman was one thing, but Callie didn't want some strange man appearing on her doorstep.

Amber grimaced and flicked her fingers. "Divorced. Which makes things even more complicated."

Callie let out a breath, feeling silly. Bad things happened in L.A., not Silverhill. Of course, she'd just witnessed a man getting shot in the back of the head....

Amber flipped open Callie's cell phone. "I'll call the B and B where I'm staying, and see if they can send a car or something. How do you manage out here without one?"

*It helps when you have your own cowboy escort service.*

"Like I said, I haven't been here long. I'll have to buy something soon."

"Probably one of those big trucks. You wouldn't happen to have the number for the Mountain View B and B, would you?"

Callie swallowed. "That's where you're staying?"

"I hope to." Amber shrugged. "My friend recommended it."

"I—I don't know the number, but I'm sure you can get it from information." Callie pursed her lips. *At least she knew Gracie Malone had a vacancy.*

Amber punched in a number and gave the name of the bed-and-breakfast. She smiled at Callie and gave her a thumbs-up sign.

Callie should probably offer the woman something to drink. Gracie's son, Charlie, could pick up Amber, but it might be a while. "Would you like a soda while you wait?"

"Sure." Amber held the phone away from her ear. "I'm going to go ahead and have information connect me. I can pay you for the call, since I know the phone service usually charges for that."

"That's okay." It would actually feel good to have someone owe *her* something for a change. She'd tried to pay back Rod for the lunch in Truth or Consequences, the shoes, the ring, the wedding, more food, and so on, but he refused.

Callie turned toward the kitchen to get a diet soda for Amber, but spun around as she heard a vehicle squeal to a stop in her driveway. Heavy boots clunked up her front steps and Rod burst through the front door.

"Callie, your father came to Silverhill."

## Chapter Nine

Callie's mouth dropped open and her face blanched. "Are you kidding me?"

"I'm not—" Rod drew up abruptly, almost tripping over the rug in front of the fireplace when he saw the dark-haired woman on the phone.

Callie's gaze darted toward the woman and then back to Rod's face. She traced a fingertip along the crease of her lips.

"Sorry." He shoved his hands in his pockets while the woman finished her call. He had no idea who she was, and he hadn't planned to blurt out the information in front of a stranger…unless this was a friend of Callie's from L.A.

She snapped the phone shut and handed it to Callie. "I'm sorry. I didn't mean to intrude here."

"I didn't realize Callie had company."

The woman laughed, a low, earthy sound. "I'm not exactly company. I ran out of gas on the road to Silverhill, and this is the first place I saw."

Callie introduced Amber to Rod, and as they shook hands, Amber said, "I can leave if you like. Looks like you have something important to discuss."

"No. I'm sure it can wait." Callie stuffed her phone into her pocket. "Is someone picking you up from the B and B?"

"Yes, but not for another hour." The woman cocked her head and a swath of dark hair fell across her cheek. "Is your ranch called Price Is Right? When I explained where I was, the woman on the phone asked me if I was at Price Is Right. Since you told me your name was Price, I figured that's where I was."

Callie nodded. "Long story, but you don't want to wait for an entire hour."

"I suppose I can walk."

"In those boots? Don't be ridiculous."

Rod ran his hands through his hair. He really wanted to talk to Callie about her father. Someone had spotted him in Silverhill, and Rod had his suspicions that he killed Bobby. But both women were looking at him with an expectant tilt to their heads.

"Where are you headed? I can give you a lift."

"The Mountain View B and B, but I don't want to put you out. They're sending someone named Charlie to pick me up."

Rod rolled his eyes. "If it's Charlie, you might be waiting for more than an hour. Did Gracie Malone say she had a vacancy?"

"A couple. Why? Is it a dump? My friend assured me it was quite pleasant and in a great location. When I mentioned it to Callie earlier, she gave me a look like I'd just announced my intention of bunking with the Manson family."

"They had an incident there this morning." Rod rubbed his hand across his chin. "More than an incident. Someone was murdered on the property."

Gasping, Amber covered her mouth. "A random thing, like there's a killer on the loose? I was just kidding about the Manson family."

"It wasn't a random shooting. The victim was involved in some shady activity."

Amber's hand slid from her mouth to cover her heart. "Do you think it's safe there? Or should I find another place?"

"I think you'll be safe, but it's up to you."

"I trust you." Amber winked at Callie. "You have that kind of face."

"He does, doesn't he?" Callie grabbed his arm, running her hand down his back.

Did his new wife-of-convenience just experience some jealousy? Amber hadn't made one flirtatious comment to him, but the woman had a seductive quality and beautiful eyes that contained a hint of wicked.

Callie shoved her hand in his back pocket. "Rod and I would be happy to give you a ride to the B and B. You can take the soda with you."

"That would be great." The woman clapped her hands and her long nails clicked together.

"Do you need to go back to your car first?" Rod held the door open for both women.

"No. I'll have the redoubtable Charlie take me to get some gas and bring me back to my car." Amber brushed past Rod, leaving a trail of exotic perfume.

When Callie reached the passenger door of Rod's truck, she swung it open and flipped the front seat forward for Amber to climb in the backseat.

ON THE WAY TO THE B AND B, Amber talked about her desire to buy a cabin in Silverhill near the ski resort, and peppered Rod with questions about the real estate in the area.

"So, do you think I can find something?"

"You should see Kerry Lindstrom. She's a Realtor, and

I've heard she's good. Gracie, the owner of your B and B, can get you the number."

Rod pulled his truck into Gracie's driveway. The yellow crime scene tape wasn't visible from here, but quite a few locals had dropped by to ogle the site. Gracie had been in her element, gossiping with people about Bobby Jingo and assuring everyone she knew he was bad from the minute he walked through her door. Right. He'd been a nice, young man minutes before someone whacked him.

He hoped that someone didn't turn out to be Jonah Price, his father-in-law.

Callie got out of the truck, while Rod idled in the driveway and flipped the seat forward for Amber. "Would you like us to wait?"

Amber clambered from the backseat, clutching her can of pop. "No. Gracie assured me she had a room. I just hope it didn't belong to the dead guy."

Rod ducked his head. "That room's off-limits for now. I'm sure she has something else for you."

"Thanks for the ride." She waved her can in the air. "And the hospitality. Hope to see both of you around while I'm house hunting."

Rod waited until Amber entered the B and B, then slid his truck into Reverse. "I don't know if this is the place for her."

"Why do you say that?" Callie snapped her seat belt in place.

"Seems a little sophisticated for Silverhill."

"Even during ski season?"

Rod shrugged. He had more important issues on his mind than some Silverhill newcomer looking for an overpriced cabin. "Don't you want to hear about your father?"

"Of course. I've had butterflies ever since you charged

into the house with the news." She folded her hands across her stomach.

"I ran into someone who saw him the night before last."

Callie's leg started bouncing. "The night before last? That's the night we arrived."

"That's right. Maybe he got here before we did." He took a swig of water from the bottle in his cup holder. "We did take that detour to Vegas."

"Is this person sure it was my father?"

"Chuck Hernandez is the owner of the Elk Ridge Lodge, and he went to high school with your father. He recognized him right away."

"Did he speak to him?"

"No. He saw him driving down the road."

"What kind of car?"

"An older-model Camaro."

Callie gasped. "That's Dad. He won that car in a bet."

"You know your father. Is he capable of killing someone?"

"Wait a minute. The bar owner saw him the night before last? Someone killed Bobby this morning. Where's he been all this time?"

"Hiding in the caves. People do it all the time. And don't forget, your father's a local."

"And his car? Do they hide cars in the caves, too?"

"Then what was he doing here, and why didn't he tell you he'd been here?"

"I don't know, Rod." She rubbed her eyes and sighed. "He's hiding something from me."

"No kidding."

Her head shot up. "Do you think he's the one who broke into the ranch?"

"Maybe. But we're back to the same question when we thought it was Bobby who had broken into the ranch. *Why?*"

"I never could figure out my father, and I don't think that's about to change now. Did your brother tell you anything more about Bobby's murder?"

"Nothing much he could share with me. The only evidence the killer left behind is the bullet lodged in Bobby's brain. Given Bobby's occupation, Rafe's going to call in the feds."

Callie snapped her fingers. "My father would have no reason to kill Bobby this morning. By then I'd already told him about my marriage and my ability to cover his debt for him. Why would he kill Bobby, just when I was ready to settle his debt?"

"Good point. Still doesn't explain what he was doing here."

"Maybe it's what we speculated about Bobby. Dad didn't know I was married and figured he needed another way to pay Bobby. So he came out to the ranch to collect what he could. He'd know better than Bobby if my grandparents had hidden any valuables at the ranch."

"Better point." He squeezed her knee, which had stopped bouncing. "You're on a roll."

"And…" She smacked the dashboard with her palms. "He didn't want to tell me, because he figured I'd accuse him of stealing from me."

"Okay. Then we're back to square one. Who killed Bobby?"

"The drug dealer Bobby was trying to muscle." The light faded from Callie's eyes and a shadow seemed to pass over her face. "And—and that has nothing to do with me, right?"

He wanted to reassure her. She'd been through so much, starting with the fire that destroyed her studio.

"Right. Your connection to Bobby is over." He slowed down and started to pull to the side of the road. "Let's head into town for some dinner."

"I just bought groceries today. I could cook."

"You cooked last night. Besides, it's time you met a few more folks in town, if you plan to make your home here." That's the first time he'd acknowledged her desire to settle in Silverhill. He'd been antsy about it before. What if he got used to the idea of having her here and she decided to head back to L.A.?

Her face brightened. "I'd like that. But can we go back to my place first, so I can freshen up and make a good impression?"

"Sure." He accelerated toward her ranch, even though the way Callie looked right now, she'd make a good impression on anyone with half a brain.

She said, "The first person I've met outside of your brother and the owner of the Miner's Café isn't even a resident."

"Who's that?"

She waved her hand behind her. "You know, Amber with the come-hither eyes."

"Is that what you call those?" He chuckled. "I have a feeling Silverhill isn't going to suit her, even in the winter, when the ski resort cranks up operations. We're strictly low-key here."

"That's what she said she wanted."

"We'll see. A lot of people visit Silverhill and take to the cozy atmosphere, only to discover the pace is too slow after the big city."

She rounded on him, her hair whipping across her face. "Is that what you think about me?"

"Whoa. Did I say that?" But she'd nailed it. He suspected Callie might fall into that category of visitor. That belief prevented him from drawing closer to her, even though that's exactly what he wanted. He wanted to bed his new wife, but could he let her go after that?

"I assure you, Rod. I have plans for that ranch—*my* ranch."

He'd be interested in hearing about those plans, but she'd just emphasized that the ranch belonged to her... not them. Most likely, she had plans that had nothing to do with him or their hasty marriage.

They returned to Price Is Right, and Callie switched her shorts for a skirt and a light sweater. She'd loosened her ponytail and her blond hair fanned across her shoulders. She'd make an even better impression now.

On the way back to Silverhill, Callie's cell phone rang and she pawed through her purse to retrieve it. "Hello?"

She let out a squeal, making him jump in his seat. "Yes, of course. Put him on."

During the pause, a smile spread across Callie's face, giving her an ethereal glow. "How are you? I miss you, too. I think about you every day and say a prayer for you every night."

Rod clutched the steering wheel. Why had Callie agreed to marry Bobby, and then him, if she already had someone she missed every day?

She laughed. "You did? That sounds fun."

Her hand groped for a tissue, and Rod plucked one for her and handed it to her. She sniffled and dabbed her eyes.

Rod clenched his jaw. This just kept getting better and better. He grabbed the bottle of water and chugged it. Why the hell had she lied to him?

"I love you. I love you. We're going to be together soon." She snapped her phone shut and blew her nose.

Grounding his teeth together, Rod growled, "Is that your boyfriend?"

She dropped the tissue and swiveled her head around. "My boyfriend? No, that was my son."

Rod choked and spewed the water he just drank all over the windshield.

She flicked a few more tissues out of the box and handed them over. *No time like the present to tell him about Jesse.*

"Your son?" He crumpled the tissues into a fist, not bothering to wipe the water dribbling from his chin.

She pried the tissues from his hand and dabbed his chin. "Well, not yet, but I'm working on it."

With Main Street within sight up ahead, Rod swerved the truck to the side of the road and threw it into Park. "Do you want to start from the beginning?"

"Sure." She owed Rod full disclosure about her life. Growing up with Mom, keeping secrets had become as natural as breathing, but Rod deserved more.

She took a deep breath. "A few years ago, I started volunteering my time teaching an art class for foster kids in the system. Nothing too complicated, just some clay figures and projects with other materials."

"I'm impressed."

"You can hold on to my application for sainthood. It was fun, and the director of the program was an attractive man…who turned out to be married, of course."

"Don't do that."

Rod's mouth, which had relaxed, now formed a thin line again.

"Do what?"

"Make light of your motivations. I'm still impressed."

Her pulse raced as she looked into his eyes. She couldn't fool Rod. She didn't want to fool Rod.

"Anyway, I met a little boy. Jesse's father had died of a drug overdose and his mother had abandoned him in a trash can." She shrugged. "We hit it off, and I applied to be a foster parent. He was with me when I lost my studio, and the county took him away from me, even though I was in the middle of the adoption process."

Rod's large hand covered hers, his calluses rough against her skin. "That's tough. You had a lot of incentive for marrying Bobby and getting the ranch. Why didn't you tell me about Jesse before?"

"I thought maybe a child would scare you off." She rolled her hand over, pressing her palm against his. "I didn't want you to think I had ulterior motives for marrying you—other than getting the ranch and getting away from Bobby."

"I probably would've been even more sympathetic." He laced his fingers through hers.

"I wouldn't use Jesse like that."

He brought her hand to his lips and kissed her wrist. The back of her throat ached at the tender gesture.

His thumb circled the warm spot left by his kiss. "Silverhill is a great place to raise kids. Are you going to get another chance with Jesse?"

She nodded. "Yeah. I contacted the Department of Child and Family Services today, and they're going to reopen our case file. I'm going to fax them some bank statements and the deed to the ranch. I might have Jesse with me as soon as this weekend, at least for a visit."

"That's great." Rod released her hand and started the engine of the truck. "Do you need me to play the doting husband and prospective father?"

"Would you?" She pushed her hair back from her face. "I don't want to lie. I won't lie to Jesse."

"We won't lie to Jesse. We're legally married. That's all the agency has to know. I won't pretend to be a father to Jesse, but how about an uncle? I've had practice with that."

She grinned. Jesse could do a lot worse for a father, but she didn't want to misrepresent the situation to him. "Okay, Uncle Rod."

Rod parked the truck across the street from a lively looking Mexican restaurant. "How old is he?"

"Five years old."

"Jesse's lucky to have you in his corner."

He jumped out of the truck and this time she stayed put, with a silly smile playing across her lips. That all went so much better than expected. She was lucky to have Rod in her corner.

Rod ushered her into the crowded restaurant with the packed bar, and several people called out to him. He waved and elbowed his way through the crowd, introducing her to the people he knew as his wife and Jonah Price's daughter.

She met a dozen people and shared some laughs before the hostess seated them at a table. After they ordered a couple of margaritas, Rod cocked his head. "You're a social person. Most folks will accept you quickly."

"It's all superficial." She flicked her fingers. "I'm good at small talk and amusing chatter. Had to be, since Mom and I moved around so much. Get in, make friends, keep things light and get out."

"Sounds like you had it down to a science."

"I did. I do."

The waitress delivered two icy margaritas, and Callie touched her tongue to the salt on the rim and then slurped some of the citrusy drink. Over the rim of her glass, she spotted Amber at the bar.

"Don't look now, but our flirtatious friend who ran out of gas is already at the bar." Callie had liked Amber well enough, until Rod showed up and the woman switched gears, an almost predatory light in her eyes.

Rod slid sideways in the booth and glanced toward the bar. "I see our resident Romeo wasted no time in getting to know our city slicker."

"That's the sheriff's deputy who came out to the shooting with Rafe." She swirled her drink and shimmied in her seat. If Rod plugged her into the local gossip, she'd really belong. "He's a Romeo?"

"Used to be. He got into a little trouble last year, and he's been a choir boy for the past several months."

She pried a little more, but Rod was no gossipmonger.

WHEN THE BILL CAME, she reached for her purse. "Let me get this so I can make a dent in what I owe you."

He slid the plastic tray toward her. "Go ahead. I'm not going to wrestle you for it."

*If only.* Callie smiled brightly and drew some bills from her wallet.

The emotions of the day had taken their toll, and Callie yawned. "Ready?"

"Yep." He slid from the booth and settled his hat on his head. "I'll take you back to your place to pick up your things for the night."

"Oh, no." She struggled from the booth feeling a little woozy…but not that woozy. She couldn't take another night under the same roof with this strong, sensitive man and not wind up in his arms. "I'll stay at my own place tonight."

"Shh." Rod took her hand and threaded his way out of the restaurant, tipping his hat to Amber on the way out, while Callie waved to her. The fresh air revived her and renewed her resolve.

They got into Rod's truck and he turned to her. "Don't be ridiculous, Callie. Your former fiancé was murdered just as you were about to pay off your dad's debt, and then the killer took a shot at you. I'm not letting you stay alone tonight."

"You said I was in the clear." She folded her hands in her lap, twisting her fingers.

"I think you are, but why take chances? If you'd rather stay at your place, I'll bunk downstairs if you have an extra toothbrush. I'm beginning to get used to traveling light."

"I don't think it's necessary. I'll be fine."

THEY DROVE THROUGH THE FRONT gate of the ranch, and Callie hopped out and latched it behind them, feeling a drop of rain on her face.

The air had been heavy all day, and Rod had predicted a summer rainstorm, complete with thunder and lightning. Callie shivered. She'd seen the lightning in New Mexico, so different from the flashes of light in Southern California. The lightning out here came down in big, scary bolts. She'd probably learn to love it.

Rod drove the truck around the back of the house, parking it next to the old toolshed.

"Why are you parking back here?"

He cut the engine but left on the headlights. "I want to check to see if you have a power saw. That porch needs to be replaced."

"Now?"

"I just thought of it. I don't want to forget tomorrow."

He jumped out of the truck, opened the toolshed and disappeared inside.

Callie trailed after him, careful not to block the light from the truck. An animal howled, and she hugged herself, rubbing her arms. She forgot sometimes how closely the wilderness surrounded the ranch.

Rod emerged from the shed and secured the door. "You don't have one. I'll bring a saw from my place tomorrow."

He locked his truck and they picked their way across the gravel toward the front of the house. She unlocked the door, and Rod stepped inside after her.

She turned. "Rod…"

He cupped her face with one hand. "I'm not leaving, Callie."

The low growl of his voice whispered across her skin. Breathless, she placed her hand on the rough denim covering his hip.

Tipping her chin up, he caressed her lips with his. She sighed into his gentle kiss, and he threaded his fingers through her hair. He pulled her tighter against his body and deepened the kiss, which turned to fire.

Her knees trembled and she wrapped her arms around his waist. His lips left her mouth and traced a burning path along her jaw. He nibbled at her ear lobe, and she gasped as his tongue darted inside her ear.

She lowered her hands to his backside, his muscles hard beneath his jeans. She arched her back as he dropped kisses down her throat.

His lips moved against her skin. "I couldn't sleep last night, imagining you in my T-shirt—and nothing else—two doors down."

He ran his thumb across her nipple and she sucked air between her teeth. "Were you only two doors away?

Wrapped in your T-shirt, I felt you next to me all night long."

"If I'd been next to you all night long, you would've felt more than a soft T-shirt against your body." He nipped her collarbone and pressed his erection against her belly.

Draping her arms around his neck, she stood on her tiptoes. He rubbed his chin across the top of her head, his stubble catching strands of her hair.

Then he swept her up in his arms and charged the stairs. "I never did get to carry you over a threshold. Will carrying you up the stairs suffice?"

"Carry me up to that bed and we'll call it even." She nuzzled his neck, feeling the low rumble of his laugh against her lips.

He nudged the door open and spun her around. "You did all this decorating today?"

"I was determined not to spend another night under your roof, snuggling a T-shirt for comfort." She kicked her legs. "How am I going to rip off your clothes when you're holding on to me like this?"

He dumped her onto the bed and yanked his T-shirt over his head. Tossing it at her, he said, "Are you ready for the real cowboy?"

Her mouth went dry and her witty repartee stuck in her throat. She knew her husband had a good body, but his flat planes of hard muscle and washboard abs left her speechless and heated her blood.

He sat down in the corner chair, dwarfing it, as he crossed one ankle over his knee and pulled off his boot. By the time he yanked off the other boot, Callie had found her voice, but her blood still hummed hot in her veins.

As he unfolded his large frame from the chair, she waved her hand, indicating his half-naked torso. "You get all those muscles working on the ranch?"

"That—and other things." He unbuckled his belt, and Callie scrambled out of her skirt and top, kicking them off the bed.

She kneeled on the bed in her underwear, arms outstretched as if to receive a wonderful gift. Rod unbuttoned his fly, giving her a glimpse of his dark blue briefs. When he reached the edge of the bed, he slipped the straps of her bra off her shoulders. His fingertip traced the swell of her breast above the white lace.

Curling her fingers over the gaping waistband of his jeans, she tugged him toward her. She splayed her hands across his chiseled chest. "Even though we've known each other less than a week, we're married. This is all legal and aboveboard, right?"

He closed his eyes and groaned as she scraped a fingernail down his midsection and hooked it in the band of his briefs. Then he captured her hand, pressed her palm against his thudding heart, and touched his forehead to hers. "It doesn't all have to be legal."

He possessed her mouth with a scorching kiss, and somehow during the inferno, she managed to lose her underwear. Cupping her bottom with his rough hands, he whispered in her ear. "This wedding night is a few days overdue. Do you want to take it nice and slow and savor the moment, or make up for lost time?"

Heck, nice and slow could come later. She yanked off his jeans and underwear and dug her fingernails into his muscled buttocks. She met his gaze and raised one eyebrow. "I married you after knowing you for a few hours. Do you think I'm the kind of girl who wants to wait for anything?"

He grinned, cowboy wicked, and she wondered what happened to her nice-guy husband. Then he disentangled himself from his jeans and scooped her up in his arms before they both tumbled onto the bed.

Tangled limbs. Hot breath. Scorching kisses. Hands and mouths everywhere.

Callie gave as good as she got and had Rod moaning, groaning and whooping.

Whooping? Must be a cowboy thing.

The storm broke outside and the storm broke inside, rolling thunder and sizzling lightning mimicking their lovemaking.

They drank their fill of each other, then lay side-by-side, panting. Callie's fingers played along the ridge of his hip, dipping into the indentation before his thighs flared to tight muscle. "About that slow and easy stuff. I think I'm ready to go there now."

Rod heaved a sigh and rolled his eyes. "I guess this is the payback for marrying a woman for her money."

She punched his shoulder and rolled on top of him, straddling his hips. "If you'd rather *not*..."

He reached up and trailed one finger from the pulse beating in her throat to the juncture where their bodies met. "I'd rather."

Closing her eyes, Callie tilted back her head, allowing her long hair to brush Rod's thighs. Her nostrils flared and her eyes flew open as she jerked forward. "Do you smell that?"

Rod sniffed. "I smell sensuous perfume, a hot woman and sex."

The blood pounded in Callie's temples and she scrambled off the bed. She knew that smell. She feared it.

She yanked back the curtains at the bedroom window and gasped.

"Fire!"

# Chapter Ten

Callie's one word acted like a cattle prod. Rod jumped out of bed and joined Callie at the window. A blaze engulfed the little wooden structure on the east end of her property. It lay too close to the main house for comfort.

"Must've been hit by lightning. And if the winds kick up, the main house might be in trouble." Rod scooped up his jeans with one hand and groped for his cell phone with the other.

He called 911 for the second time today and reported the fire. "Let's get out of the house just in case, and I'll see if I can find a hose."

He didn't have to tell Callie twice. Her blue eyes looked huge in her pale face as she tugged her skirt over her hips. Spinning around, she banged her shin on the chest at the foot of the bed and tumbled to the floor.

Rod crouched down to help her up and a hot tear splashed on his hand. "You're okay, sweetheart. We have plenty of time to get out of here."

He rubbed the red spot on her shin as she scrambled to her feet.

Her voice rose to near hysteria. "We have to get out of here. Now."

Damn. He'd forgotten. She'd already lost everything

in a fire. She must be terrified. He grabbed her hand. "Let's go."

The acrid scent of the fire hit him as he burst out the front door. The blaze crackled fiercely, unabated by the light rain. Silverhill had its own fire department, and it had a good response time.

The heat of the flames warmed his face, and he pulled Callie toward the front gate. Now that she was outside, her frantic pace had ceased and she seemed almost frozen in her fear.

Hugging Callie, Rod shielded her from the flames. He whispered soothing words into her hair. He'd wanted to find a hose to get some water on the fire, but Callie needed him more. The structure could burn.

Her tense muscles relaxed when the sirens of the fire trucks wailed down the road. Rod kissed the top of her head. "They're here. It's going to be fine. The fire didn't come anywhere near the house."

She nodded and lifted her face from where she'd pressed it against his chest. "I'm sorry to be such a wimp about this. It's just that…"

He stroked her hair down her back. "I know. You've been through this before."

The firemen got to work, and Rod watched the stream of water through narrowed eyes. "How did it start?"

She lifted her shoulders. "Didn't you say lightning?"

"Not this fire. The one in L.A."

Her eyes widened and the orange-and-red glow from the flames flickered in her eyes. "It—it was a faulty gas-powered water heater. Jesse was with me then, but thank God he was at a sleepover that night. The water heater exploded. Even though it was midnight, I was working in my studio, which probably saved my life."

"How so?" He didn't want to scare her, but most people

never experienced even one fire in their lives. This was an odd coincidence.

"My studio was set behind the main house, which was a rental house. The fire spread quickly through the house, but when I heard the explosion I fled my studio. It leapt to the roof of the studio, destroying that, too, but I'd gotten out safely."

He hugged her tighter. "Thank God for the eccentric work habits of artists."

"Why did you ask that?" She pulled away from him.

"Just seems like a coincidence." He plucked at a strand of hair clinging to her lashes.

"Are you implying I have some psycho after me, setting fires?"

"No." Although the thought had crossed his mind. "You didn't even know the existence of Bobby Jingo at the time of the first fire, did you?"

She gasped and stepped back. "Do you think this—" she waved her arm at the quickly diminishing fire "—has anything to do with Bobby and the money and his murder?"

"Did you know him then?" A muscle ticked in Rod's jaw. Did the reasons for Bobby's proposal go deeper than just the money?

"No." She smoothed her hair back from her face. "When that water heater blew in L.A., I'd never heard of Bobby Jingo before in my life."

Rod let out a long breath. "Then this was probably the lightning."

Judd Cramer, one of the firemen, approached them, his boots crunching the gravel. "Hey, Rod. I hope you two weren't planning on using that structure for anything. It'll have to be demolished."

Rod introduced Judd to Callie and she crossed her

arms. "Well, I did have some plans for it, but I guess I'll have to change those. How'd the fire start?"

"Probably the lightning."

Rod blew out another breath.

Judd continued, "There were quite a few combustibles in that building—some paint thinner, lighter fluid—all it took was a spark. We'll do a more through investigation when it cools down. Are you planning to keep the ranch?"

His gaze darted from Rod to Callie, not knowing whom to address.

Callie said, "Yes."

"Then it might be a good idea to give the place a complete inspection. I know it's been vacant for a while, with just those caretakers looking after it. You don't know what fire hazards and other dangers might be lurking on the property."

"We'll check it out. Thanks, Judd." Rod held out his hand and Judd's large, soot-covered glove enveloped it.

As they watched the firemen clean up, Rod wrapped his arms around Callie, pulling her back so that her shoulder blades rested against his chest.

A tremble rolled through her body. "I was hoping to turn that into a studio. I guess that's two studios down the drain, or rather up in flames."

"You can build something better, more stable." His hands traveled along her arms and he massaged her shoulders.

She rubbed her cheek against the back of his hand. "That's a coincidence, isn't it? Two fires in the past six months."

"Yeah." He blinked at the smoldering embers of the fire. "Coincidence."

TWO DAYS LATER, CALLIE STOOD at the edge of the cleared patch of land, with her hands on her hips and a satisfied smile curving her lips. Having access to money soothed all the little hiccups of life.

Rod had given her a recommendation for a company—a man and his son really—and they'd come out and demolished the remainder of the burnt-out shack, hauled away the mess and raked over the land. Next, she intended to call a builder and discuss plans for a new studio.

Even more exciting news had come her way. DCFS had called her yesterday, and a social worker was flying out with Jesse this weekend for an extended visit.

"Hello."

The voice startled Callie out of her pleasant thoughts and she turned toward the gate. Amber, dressed in skinny jeans and high heels, waved.

Callie opened the gate for her, frowning at the heels. "My drive isn't paved yet. I don't want you to ruin your heels."

"These old things?" Amber kicked a foot out in front of her, shaking it back and forth. "This is my country wear."

Callie shook her head. "Any luck yet?"

Amber tucked a lock of dark hair behind her ear. "That sheriff's deputy from the other night told me he's swearing off women for a while. Who does that?"

Callie snorted. "I meant with the house hunting."

"Oh, that." Amber laughed. "I've looked at a few places, but now I'm thinking I might want one of those condos closer to the ski lifts."

"Would you like something to drink?"

"Unless you can whip up a Bloody Mary, I'm good." She pointed a manicured finger at the patch of land. "I heard you had some excitement the other night."

Callie swallowed. Even though the fire hadn't come close to the house, she'd had a nightmare about it last night. She woke up in Rod's arms, and her fear melted away immediately.

"The lightning ignited some combustibles in the shed, and the whole thing burst into flames."

"You managed to take care of it quickly, or is that your hardworking husband's doing?"

"Rod has enough to do at his own ranch. I hired someone to clear out the mess."

"Visitors this weekend?"

Folding her arms, Callie pursed her lips into a thin line. For an outsider, Amber sure seemed plugged into the party line—and a little too interested in Rod.

"I'm sorry." Amber covered her mouth. "It's that Gracie Malone. She's such a gossip. She told me you're expecting a visit from a little boy this weekend."

Rod hadn't been kidding about the small-town grapevine. They'd been having lunch at the Miner's Café the day before, when Callie got the call from DCFS about Jesse. She'd been too excited to keep her mouth shut.

Well, she wanted to jump into the local atmosphere headfirst, didn't she? Guess she had to accept the good with the bad.

Callie unclenched her hands. "Funny how word spreads around these small towns, isn't it? I suppose, as a seasonal resident, you won't be subjected to it as much."

"I hope not." Amber wrinkled her nose. "I like my privacy."

"Did you come by for a specific reason, or just to chat? Do you want to come inside?" Just Callie's luck. The friendliest person in Silverhill didn't even live here.

Amber checked her watch. "I have an appointment with

my Realtor. I just came by to find out if you wanted to have dinner tonight."

"I'm sorry. I'm having dinner with Rod's brother and his wife. She's in town for the weekend."

"She's the FBI agent, isn't she?" Amber dabbed at her lipstick with her fingertip.

Callie laughed. "You'd better be careful or you'll wind up sitting in matching rocking chairs with Gracie, trading gossip."

Amber smacked her forehead. "Oh, my God. That image is enough to drive me back to Aspen."

"You're going to Aspen?" Rod strode across the property, sweat beading his brow, his T-shirt tucked under his arm.

Callie's fingers tingled as she recalled running them across the slabs of shifting muscles on Rod's bare chest. She shot a glance beneath her lashes at Amber, whose dark eyes glittered with desire—or something.

"Where'd you come from?" Callie moved forward, preventing Amber's greedy gaze from scorching her husband.

With perhaps the same thought in his mind, Rod shook out his wrinkled T-shirt, removed his hat and pulled the shirt over his head.

"I was doing some work on my side of the property, and saw that your fence needed some mending, so I got that done."

Amber cocked her head. "So, are you two going to join up properties? How copacetic for…both of you. Did you have one of those marriages arranged in the cradle?"

A muscle pulsed in Rod's jaw as he put his black hat back on, pulling it over his eyes. "How's it working out with Kerry? Have you seen anything you like, or are you ready to find tonier digs?"

"Kerry's a doll. She's showing me some condos this afternoon, so I'd better get going and leave you two newlyweds alone." She sashayed down the drive, picking her way carefully over the gravel, with her high heels wobbling.

"What did she want?"

"She wanted to get together for dinner."

"You told her you had plans?"

"Of course."

Rubbing his chin, Rod stared at the gate long after Amber disappeared. "She sure is friendly."

"To you." Callie jabbed him in the ribs.

Rod grabbed her hand and kissed her fingers. "Flirting is second nature to a woman like that. She sees a man. She flirts. I don't think her quarry matters to her."

"Yeah, until she got a load of your pecs." She ran her hands across his chest, his damp shirt conforming to his muscles. She didn't blame Amber for flirting with Rod.

"She's friendly to you, too."

"I think it's because I'm the first person she ran into in Silverhill, and we helped her out. Maybe it's because we're both city girls and a little out of our element."

Rod's green eyes darkened and his brows collided over his nose. "Do you feel like you're going to have a problem fitting in here?"

Her heart skipped a beat. Did he really care? "I haven't been here long enough to tell. I've been too busy around the ranch to meet many people."

He kissed her, his lips warm and inviting. "You'll have another chance with Rafe tonight at dinner, and I know you'll like his wife, Dana. I'm going back to my own place to finish what I started this morning before your broken fence distracted me."

"Is that all that can distract you?" She fluffed his hair

out of his eyes and pouted with her lower lip in a parody of Amber's flirtatious techniques.

"You're plenty distracting." He nuzzled her neck, tickling her collarbone with the tip of his tongue.

She giggled and smacked his shoulder. "That tickles. Get to work and I'll see you at dinnertime. I'm still working on Jesse's room."

He kissed her again and left the way he came, through the back of her property, where it hooked up with his.

She stood for a moment, clasping her hands in front of her. What happened to taking it slow, until she could ascertain Rod's true intentions? A tidal wave of desire and need had swept them along in its sudden fury, blinding them to their earlier promises. Or at least it had swept her away.

What had Amber said? Copacetic?

PROMPTLY, AT SIX FORTY-FIVE, Rod drove his truck through Callie's gate. Before he could cut the engine, she flew down the front steps, a gauzy skirt swirling around her legs, blond hair shimmering down her back. She looked every inch the artist.

She yanked open the passenger door and hopped onto the seat, infusing his truck with the scent of lilacs. She held up a bottle of wine in a bag. "Do the sheriff and FBI agent drink wine?"

"Probably not on duty."

She crossed her legs and tapped one foot against the other as she punched the buttons on the radio.

"You nervous?" He slid his hand over hers.

"A little. I never had much family. My mom's people pretty much disowned her because she had a bad habit of stealing from them whenever they got together. And you probably know my dad's history better than I do."

"Nothing to it. Avoid discussing politics, religion and money, and make sure you compliment their kids."

"You don't fool me, Rod McClintock." She wagged her finger at him. "I can tell you and Rafe have a good relationship. It must've been nice growing up with siblings. I often wished I had someone to help carry the burden of my parents."

"Are you going to give Jesse a sibling?" As soon as the words left his mouth, he realized they sounded wrong. He'd been taking a lot for granted since they slept together. He'd planned on waiting it out until Callie decided what she wanted. Now he was asking her about siblings for her adopted son. "I mean…"

She turned her head to look out the window, as if she hadn't heard him. "I'd like to."

He kept his mouth shut the rest of the way to Rafe's little mountain retreat, and Callie didn't seem inclined to start up a conversation. Maybe they'd both come to the realization that they were taking things too fast.

He pulled into Rafe's driveway behind Dana's car and doused his headlights. "Are you ready?"

"As ready as I'll ever be."

As they walked up to the front door, Rod's shoulder brushed Callie's arm and they both stiffened.

They'd rushed their relationship. And Callie knew it, too.

Dana opened the door and hugged Rod before holding him at arm's length. "I never believed I'd see the day."

Rod introduced Dana to Callie, and Dana studied her with her dark eyes. Rod made a slicing motion with his hand across his throat. Dana had better not spring any surprises on Callie tonight.

She enfolded Callie in her arms, dark head against blond. "It's so nice to meet you. I can tell you all of Rod's embarrassing secrets if you like. I'm not just his sister-in-law, but I grew up in Silverhill, too."

Rafe joined them and made a big deal out of meeting Callie properly. He winked at her. "I almost arrested Callie."

"I heard all about it." Dana rolled her eyes at Callie. "I'm sure it must've been a shock to find out Rod owned the ranch next to yours. I can't get over the coincidence."

"Yeah, I've had a lot of those in my life lately." Callie twisted her hair and tossed it over her shoulder.

Did he hear doubt in her voice again? He deserved it. Any sensible woman would have her suspicions about him after he took her to bed.

Tension stretched between him and Callie during dinner, but she seemed to get along well with Rafe and Dana. As usual, Rafe turned on the charm and Callie fell under his spell. Dana seemed almost giddy, and Rod flashed more than a few warning signs her way.

Dinner wound down, and they headed for the living room for coffee and dessert.

A car rolled to a stop outside the house, headlights illuminating the yard. Dana pulled the curtain aside. "It's Kelsey, our daughter. Her friend's family took the girls to see a movie in Durango."

Dana opened the door, and Kelsey entered the room chattering about the movie. She stopped when she saw Callie. She ran toward her and tumbled into a heap at her feet. "Are you my aunt Callie?"

Callie smiled. "I suppose I am. You have beautiful hair. I think it's longer than mine."

Rod's throat tightened, and he threw a wild look at Rafe, who shrugged.

Dana followed her daughter and gathered her hair into

a ponytail and playfully yanked on it. "Of course she's your aunt Callie. She's married to your uncle Rod."

Kelsey threw her head back and laughed. "Then she's a double aunt."

Dana coughed. "Do you want some pie?"

"What's a double aunt?" Callie tilted her head, a half smile curving her lips.

"You're married to my Uncle Rod, Dad's brother, and you're also Mom's sister."

All the adults in the room gasped, and Callie felt as if they'd sucked the air from her lungs. What was Kelsey talking about?

Dana wailed, "Rafe."

Rafe held up his hands. "I didn't say anything."

Kelsey's dark brows created a V over her straight little nose. "Dad didn't tell me, but I heard you talking about her last night." She placed her hands on Callie's knees. "I was so excited to have another aunt. Is—is that okay?"

The poor girl probably felt the adults' displeasure, since it covered the room like a wet blanket. Callie patted Kelsey's hands. "Of course it's okay. I've never had a niece before."

Callie couldn't believe the words had come out in a normal tone, since she was screaming in her head. She had a sister? This woman, Rod's sister-in-law, was her *sister?* Dana had said she grew up in Silverhill. She had to be Dad's daughter. Of course. Dana was tall and dark, probably Native American. Leave it to Dad.

Leave it to Rod to tell her nothing. Just like he'd neglected to tell her he owned the ranch next to hers. How did she ever think she could trust him?

The voices continued to rise and fall around her, and she realized Kelsey's parents had convinced the child to go to bed. Kelsey held out her small hand. "It was nice to meet you, Aunt Callie. I hope we can be friends."

"I hope so, too." She smoothed Kelsey's hair and tucked it behind her ear.

Once Kelsey said good-night to everyone, turned down the hallway and shut a door, Callie jumped from her chair. "I have to get out of here."

"I'm sorry." Dana reached out. "I didn't want you to find out this way."

With tears stinging her eyes, Callie brushed past Dana. What else was Rod keeping from her?

She stumbled down the front steps and marched toward the road, clutching her purse to her side. She couldn't walk all the way back to Price Is Right, especially since Rafe's house was practically stashed in the wilderness, but she had a cell phone. Did taxis operate in small towns like Silverhill? Maybe she could call her new best friend, Amber.

"Callie!"

Rod's voice behind her put a hitch in her step, but she continued tromping down the dark road.

"Callie, wait."

She straightened her back and continued. She'd planned on giving Rod a chance to prove he didn't want her ranch, but then she'd foolishly fallen for him, giving him an easy pass...and easy access to her bed.

He caught up with her and grabbed her arm. She tried to shake him off, but his grip tightened.

"I'm sorry I didn't tell you about Dana. I didn't figure you needed any more drama in your life right now, and Dana's not even positive you are sisters."

"She seemed positive in there." She jerked her chin toward the house.

"Her great-aunt told her Jonah Price was her father, but

she has no real proof. After meeting you, she probably wishes for it even more."

"Don't patronize me." She pulled away from him, but planted her feet on the ground.

"Like you, Dana was an only child. She didn't know her father and only recently discovered he might be Jonah. She's anxious to connect with you, but she hadn't planned to broach the subject for a while, until you got settled."

"Why didn't someone tell me? Why did I have to find out from that precious little girl?"

"I told you, sweetheart. You have enough on your plate right now."

She kicked a pebble on the ground. "It's not like having a sibling is a bad thing. You don't know how many times I wished I had a sister or brother. I don't like it when you... when *people* keep things from me."

"I know, and it seems like I've been doing a lot of that." He took her hand and tugged. "I'll take you home."

She snatched her hand back but followed him to the truck. Settling on the seat, she asked, "Do Rafe and Dana think I'm rude?"

"Rude?" He backed up and rolled onto the road. "No way. Dana feels bad that Kelsey overheard them and spilled the beans. She understands what a shock it must be to you, especially after..."

"After?" Callie gathered the material of her skirt in her fists.

"You know." Rod accelerated and frowned in his rearview mirror. "After that other discovery."

Callie clasped her hands between her knees to keep them still. "So I met a man in the middle of New Mexico who not only owned the ranch next to my grandfather's ranch, but whose brother was married to my sister...half sister."

The truck lurched and Rod grasped the steering wheel. "This thing needs a tune-up. Yeah, half sister. If it makes you feel any better, I have a half brother I've never met."

"I just feel so confused, Rod." She massaged her temples. "I have to tell you, the idea occurred to me that I'm in the middle of some huge McClintock family plot to steal my ranch."

His brows shot up, but he kept his eyes on the road. "Is that what you're worried about? The money?"

"The money?" She grabbed the armrest as the truck listed to the right.

"All your grandfather's dough. Are you afraid Dana's going to try to make some claim on it?"

Callie's jaw dropped as a flash of heat claimed her body. "I didn't even think of that."

Rod cursed and struggled with the steering wheel.

As the truck skidded toward the embankment, Callie gasped and gripped the edges of her seat. "What are you doing?"

Then she screamed as the truck spun out of control.

## Chapter Eleven

The truck dipped in the front and rocked. Rod fought to control the jerking, shuddering vehicle, and Callie squeezed her eyes shut, waiting for the inevitable impact. She only hoped it didn't come at the bottom of a ravine.

After what seemed like an hour, the truck smacked against something hard and huffed to a stop. Heavy breathing echoed in the cab of the truck and Callie peeled one eye open.

The road in front of them had disappeared, and the starry night sky stretched before them.

Rod hissed through clenched teeth, "Don't move. Our front end is hanging over the edge of a cliff."

Callie held her breath, as if one puff of air could send them into oblivion. For all she knew, it could.

"What happened? Did we hit something?"

"I don't know. The truck was acting funny as soon as we picked up speed." He snapped the door handle, and she grabbed his arm as the truck rocked.

"Where are you going?"

"I'm going to get us out of this mess."

Callie lifted her purse from the floor with one finger. "I'll call 911."

"You do that, but I don't want them to find us at the

bottom of this mountain when they get here…or in a flaming vehicle, or both."

Callie sniffed and smelled brake fluid, burning rubber… and smoke. Her heart hammered in her chest.

Rod pushed the door open slowly, but the truck creaked and tipped forward. Callie squeaked in the middle of her conversation with the operator, and then asked Rod where they where located.

He told her while he unsnapped his seat belt. "I'm going to crawl in the back and exit that way. We should be okay with the weight in the back."

"As long as we don't dislodge any rocks that might be holding us in place." She was all for waiting for the emergency rescue, but Rod was a man of action. The smell of smoke infiltrating the car indicated they might not have enough time to wait for the fire engines this time.

He squeezed into the backseat, and the truck tilted back with him.

"That's a good sign." She let out a long breath.

Callie removed her seat belt, too, in case she had to jump out of the truck in a hurry.

Rod clicked open the back door. The truck remained steady, but Callie could smell gasoline, and her pulse galloped.

When Rod stepped outside the truck, a wave of panic crashed over Callie and she clenched a fist to her mouth to keep from flailing about the truck and sending it over the cliff.

"It's okay, Callie. You're going to be fine. Stay put. I'm coming to get you."

Her breath came out in pants as she pressed her back against the leather seat. Rod's face appeared at her window and she sobbed in relief. He pointed to the lock, and she clicked the lock button. Easing the door open, he said, "Steady. Don't step down. Just come into my arms."

She flew from her seat against his chest and he dragged her back, just as the sirens sounded. She clung to him and he lifted her in his arms, cradling her as he took long, loping steps away from the truck.

An explosion rocked the ground and Rod lurched forward, taking her with him. They thudded against the asphalt, as a crash followed the explosion.

Callie peeked over Rod's shoulder, digging her nails into his back. "Oh my God. It's gone."

He jerked his head up, the lights from the fire truck bathing his face in a red glow. He closed his eyes and crushed Callie against his sweat-soaked T-shirt.

Several seconds later, a fireman hunched over them, his gear rustling and clanking. "Are you folks okay? The vehicle went over the edge."

Rod struggled to sit up, still clamping her to his body, as if he feared she'd fall off the cliff with the truck. "We're fine. I think we got out just in time. The truck exploded before it launched over the side."

"We saw the explosion. The ambulance just arrived. I'm going to leave you to the EMTs while we douse the fire."

They both refused a stretcher, so the EMTs had them sit on the back of the ambulance while they checked their vitals. The only injuries they had were a few cuts and scrapes, incurred when they fell on the ground after the explosion.

When the EMTs finished with their bandages, Callie murmured in Rod's ear. "So what happened?"

"I'm not sure. It was either something mechanical or the tire blew."

Her gaze wandered to the side of the road where the

firemen were extinguishing a few small blazes on the hillside below. "Do you think there will be enough of your truck left to tell us?"

He rubbed his face and shrugged. "I don't know. I just thank God you weren't in that truck when it went over."

"And I thank you." She rubbed her palm along his cheek. "If we'd waited for the firemen, it would've been too late...for both of us."

Rod ran his hands through his hair and clutched the back of his neck. "Are you normally accident-prone, Callie?"

"No." She picked at the edge of one of the bandages on her elbow. "But this was one heck of an accident."

"Was it?"

"What are you saying?" But she knew exactly what he was saying. Why were these things happening to her? A fire at her ranch, and now a potentially lethal car accident.

"You've been the victim of two fires, and now a car accident, in under a year, not to mention a target for both Bobby's goons and his killer. What's going on?"

She jumped off the ambulance. "That earlier fire in L.A. has nothing to do with any of this. I'd never heard of Bobby Jingo then. And I have no idea why someone would be after me because of Bobby. I'm ready and willing to pay back the money my father owes. All someone has to do is contact me, not kill me."

"What was your father doing in Silverhill?"

"I don't know. I can't reach him." She put her hands over her ears. "Stop. I'm not in any danger. These are all coincidences...just like running into you in New Mexico."

He hoisted himself up and put an arm around her. "I'm

not trying to upset you. Just trying to look at this from a logical standpoint."

"Well, there's nothing logical about it. Any of it." She pointed to a policeman approaching them. "I think he wants to ask us some questions. And I don't think he's interested in wild speculations."

"I'll give him just the facts, ma'am."

Callie hugged herself as Rod strode toward the cop, hand outstretched. If she was in danger, wouldn't that put Jesse in danger, too? Should she cancel his trip this weekend?

The thought caused a sharp pain to slice through her chest. Jesse was already at risk in the foster care system. She could protect him better here.

She studied Rod through narrowed eyes. And Rod could protect them both.

THE FOLLOWING DAY, CALLIE LEFT Rod to straighten out the insurance on his truck. Rod and his truck had been her saviors that day in New Mexico as she fled the wedding. She was going to miss the big behemoth…the truck, not Rod.

So far, the accident investigators hadn't been able to determine whether or not the truck had a mechanical failure, and the weather couldn't have caused the accident. The water from the rainstorm the previous night had already evaporated from the road.

Most likely, given Rod's description of the truck's behavior before he lost control of it, a wheel had come loose. They happened to be in the wrong place at the wrong time.

Just an accident.

Now they both had rental cars. Callie tapped the dashboard of the Ford she'd rented that morning. She didn't want to keep depending on Rod for rides everywhere, even before he lost his truck.

After the news about Dana, Callie's trust in Rod ebbed. Then he saved her from the burning truck and her trust flowed back. She'd decided they needed to keep their distance for a while, at least emotionally. For all she knew, Rod's programming to do the right thing was fueling his attraction to her.

And her attraction to him? Maybe her longing for a home and roots was fueling her attraction.

That, and his tight jeans.

She cruised into Durango with the intent of settling more business matters. She had a meeting with Doug Smyth and planned to set up some accounts at the bank.

As she and Doug wrapped up their meeting, Callie pawed through her purse for her sunglasses. "Doug, what would happen to the ranch and all of my grandfather's assets if I died?"

Smyth glanced up from his computer screen, blinking. "It would all revert to Grady Pierce...unless you had a will or trust. Good question. I'll get working on a living trust for you, and we can review the details later. Nobody should be without a will, even a young, healthy woman like you, Callie."

*Young, healthy—and accident-prone.*

After leaving Smyth's office, she walked the two blocks to the Bank of Colorado. She slipped into its air-conditioned confines and almost plowed into the solid form of Grady Pierce—the man who had just been on her mind.

He held up his hands, clutching a deposit slip. "Well, if it isn't Silverhill's newest rancher. I'll bet McClintock's doing all he can to make a smooth transition from his property to yours."

Callie held up her middle finger and brushed past him, their close contact sending a shiver down her spine. Could Grady be anxious enough to get her ranch to kill for it?

His booming laugh echoed after her, and she shrugged off her concern. The man was a buffoon.

The bank manager, Andrew Dawson, waved her over to his glass-encased cubicle. She settled into a chair across from his desk and pulled some forms from her purse.

As THEY NEARED THE CLOSE of their business, Andrew shoved a card across the desk toward her. "Your grandfather also had a safe deposit box. Do you want to check that out today?"

"Mr. Smyth mentioned that earlier, and I forgot about it. What do I have to do?" If Grandpa Ennis had more riches stashed away in this safe deposit box, she'd have more to share with Dana—her sister. It seemed only fair that Dana should take half of the inheritance if it turned out she had Price blood running through her veins.

Rod's accusation that she'd balked at having a sister because of the money really hit below the belt.

Andrew tapped the card on the desk. "Fill out this signature card and I'll turn over a key to you. We keep a guard key, and you and another bank employee must be present to open the box."

Callie scrawled her signature on the card and shoved it back to Andrew. He asked her to wait by a door while he went to another area of the bank. He returned with two keys and gave one to her. "That's yours to keep. Bring it with you every time you wish to access the box."

He unlocked the door onto a stairway, and Callie followed him into the basement of the bank. At the bottom of the stairs they faced a lead door. Andrew entered a code on the security pad and spun the large handle to open the door.

"Wow, it's like Fort Knox down here."

"We keep our boxes secure."

She followed him into the carpeted room lined with rows of metal boxes in different sizes. He led her down one row, checking the card for the box number. They stopped in front of a wall of large boxes.

"It's number 586."

He inserted his key into the box and invited her to do the same. The small lock clicked, and Andrew slid the box from its cubby and placed it on the table behind them.

He then turned and walked out of the room. "Press this button by the side of the door when you're finished. I'll be waiting right outside."

The heavy door slammed behind him, and a lock clicked into place. Whew, now she really felt important.

Holding her breath, Callie slid the lid from the box. Glittering jewels and gold coins did not meet her curious gaze. She shuffled through some old papers and documents and a couple of passports, flicking one open.

Her grandmother's smiling face appeared on the passport and Callie choked on bitter regret. She traced her finger across the picture and whispered, "Why didn't you rescue me?"

Blinking her eyes, she dug through the rest of the box. Birth certificates. Marriage license. Passports. She pinched a yellowed envelope between two fingers and reached inside. She pulled out a folded piece of wrinkled paper and smoothed it on the table.

She recognized her father's writing, even in its childish form. He'd printed the words "Treasure Map" across the top of the paper and had drawn a dotted line, squiggling around the property of Price Is Right.

Callie smiled. She hadn't realized her father had been so fanciful, and his parents had saved it. She carefully creased the map, slid it back inside the envelope and dropped it in her purse. She and Jesse might have some fun with that.

She replaced the remaining documents back in the box and slid it home. After she locked the box, she pressed the button to summon Andrew.

Once outside, she took deep gulps of fresh air. The vault had been stuffy and uncomfortable. She'd almost felt like she was prying into her grandparents' lives. Strangers' lives, even though they were family.

With Jesse coming tomorrow, and a half sister in town, maybe she'd just get that family after all. And she'd keep them close…and safe.

"REALLY, ROD, YOU DON'T NEED to take me. I have my own rental car now," Callie protested, but a warm glow had spread from her head to her toes when Rod had driven up to the ranch to take her to Durango to pick up Jesse at the airport.

"You mean you don't trust my driving after that one little accident?" He folded his arms and leaned against the railing on the porch that he'd just fixed the other day.

Rolling her eyes, she pulled the door closed behind her. "That was not little. Did the cops come up with a reason for the accident yet?"

He hoisted his shoulder from the post. "Looks like the back wheel came loose."

She shivered as goose bumps raced up her arms. "Scary." Catching his narrowed gaze, she straightened her shoulders and charged down the porch steps. "But they're calling it an accident, aren't they?"

"For now."

He opened the passenger door of his rental and she slid onto the seat. She snapped her seat belt into place as Rod pulled away from the ranch.

Rod cleared his throat. "Dana wants to talk with you. She's going to get a DNA test done to find out if she's really Jonah Price's daughter. Her great-aunt told her she was, but she's never gotten proof and she never contacted Jonah."

"She doesn't need my permission to do that." Callie folded her hands in her lap to stop their trembling. Looked like Dana really wanted to pursue this sister thing.

"The lab will need your DNA to confirm a match. Are you okay with that?"

Callie dropped her head, allowing her hair to shield her face and the ridiculous smile that pulled at her lips. Dana probably wanted to take a crack at the Price inheritance. What would she possibly want with a sister? She already had family, including some wonderful great-aunt who'd raised her.

She whipped back her hair and shrugged. "Sure. If it turns out she is my father's daughter, I plan to cut her in on the money."

"She's not interested in that, Callie. Dana grew up without a father or siblings. I think she's excited by the prospect of having a sister, especially since—" Rod broke off as color rushed into his face.

"Especially since that sister is married to her husband's brother?" She snorted. "We both know that's a joke— don't we?"

Rod's gaze drilled the highway. "About that night of the fire…"

She held up her hands. "That was a mistake. We got carried away. Now that Jesse is here, we can resume our platonic marriage."

Rod nodded, his jaw tight, and Callie turned to look out the window, tears stinging her eyes. Truth was, she'd been longing to feel Rod's strong, warm body pressed against hers ever since they'd made love. That had been the real fire that night.

But she didn't want to complicate their arrangement. She didn't want to get her hopes up, only to have them dashed to pieces.

They drove to Durango in silence. Without his classical CDs, which had plunged to a fiery demise along with his truck, Rod had punched in a country music station and was tapping his thumbs on the steering wheel in time to the music.

This music obviously didn't have the same soothing effect on him. One of her sculptures could look a lot softer than Rod's face, which seemed etched in granite. Had her comment about their platonic marriage irritated him?

*Yeah, because the sex had been out of this world, genius.*

Rod finally pulled into the small parking lot of the Durango-La Plata County Airport and Callie almost tumbled from the car in her eagerness to see Jesse. They watched his plane land, and Callie's heart somersaulted when she saw him disembark, a small backpack on his back, clutching the social worker's hand.

As Rod waited by the exit, Callie waved her arms, even though it would've been tough for Jesse to miss her. A wide grin claimed his face, and he broke away from his chaperone and ran toward Callie.

Callie grabbed him and swung him around, swallowing around the large lump in her throat. She kissed his cheeks, and he was still young enough that he didn't mind.

Jesse grabbed a handful of Callie's skirt while she dug through her purse to show her ID to Linda Fisk, the social worker. She'd be coming out to the ranch to look things over before leaving Jesse there and flying back to L.A. the next day.

Callie had every intention of making a first-rate impression to make this visit a permanent one.

"Do we need to wait for your bags?"

Linda shook her head and pointed to a small suitcase on wheels, with a duffel bag bunched up on top of it. "We took our luggage on the plane."

Callie gulped again, realizing Jesse had very little in this world. All that was about to change.

Holding Jesse's hand, she turned toward the exit and almost tripped over her feet when she caught a glimpse of Rod by the door, his black cowboy hat clutched under his arm.

She had some explaining to do. She'd told the agency in L.A. that she'd gotten married, and frankly, they'd sounded pleased to hear the news. Now she realized Linda would expect a newly married couple to be living together. If Linda suspected some kind of sham marriage, she might think Callie was using it as a ploy to adopt Jesse.

She took a deep breath and strode toward Rod. "Linda, this is Rod McClintock—my husband. Rod, Linda Fisk, the social worker from the agency."

As they shook hands, Linda practically beamed.

Jesse tugged on Callie's hand, and she looked down. "What is it, sweetie?"

Jesse's big brown eyes had grown even bigger as he pointed a small finger at Rod. "Is he going to be my new daddy?"

# Chapter Twelve

Callie choked, so Rod figured he'd better take over. He crouched next to the little boy and tapped his chest. "That's right, pardner. Is that okay with you?"

Jesse's mouth dropped open as he nodded. "Are you a cowboy?"

"Yep. Do you want to learn how to ride a horse? I don't think Callie's going to be able to help you with that."

Jesse covered his mouth and giggled.

The social worker clapped her hands. "This is wonderful. It's so nice to see you settled, Callie…Mrs. McClintock."

Callie's blue eyes darkened and her pert nose practically twitched. "Wonderful."

Rod stretched to his full height, hooking one thumb in his belt loop. "Callie and I have two ranches, right next to each other. It's a lot of work. Do you think you can help me, Jesse?"

"Yep." Jesse hooked his thumbs in the pockets of his blue jeans and Rod patted his shoulder.

Callie's lips formed a thin, tight line, so Rod patted her shoulder, too. What did she expect? She'd told the adoption agency she'd gotten married. She must've realized the social worker wouldn't look too kindly upon a marriage of convenience. He was just playing his part, even though she wanted to return to their platonic relationship.

Now Callie would have to spend the night with him tonight, under the watchful eyes of Linda Fisk. *Let's see how long platonic lasts.*

They piled into the rental car and Callie kept up a stream of bright chatter. The little boy adored her. And why wouldn't he? Callie's animated demeanor and frequent laughter could brighten anyone's world.

She'd brightened his.

But a boy couldn't be raised by a Disneyland mom, full of fun and games every minute of the day. A boy needed structure and discipline. A boy needed a father.

When they pulled to a stop in front of the ranch house, Jesse scampered out of the car and ran in circles.

As Linda followed him out of the car, she laughed over her shoulder. "He's been waiting a long time to stretch his legs."

The car door slammed and Callie whipped around. "What exactly do you think you're doing?"

"Me?" Rod raised his brows in feigned innocence.

"'Little cowpoke' this and 'pardner' that, pretending to be Jesse's father." She tossed back her hair.

"And what would you suggest? 'No, Jesse, I'm not going to be your father'? 'I just married Callie because I picked her up on the side of the road in a bedraggled wedding dress after she ran out on her wedding to a loan shark who's just been murdered'? Linda would've snatched that boy back and loaded him back on the plane like *that*." He snapped his fingers.

She collapsed back in her seat, biting her lip. "You're right. This is a mess."

"Why is it a mess?"

Jerking her thumb toward Jesse, hanging over a fence

pointing at a hawk, she said, "Did you notice the way he looked at you? All adoration and admiration. He's going to be so disappointed when he finally figures out you're not his new dad."

Rod took her hand and smoothed his thumb across her knuckles. "I can still be his dad. Even if…*when* our marriage settles back into what it is—a marriage of convenience—I'll still be right next door. I can teach Jesse to ride and rope, and all those other cowboy things at which you're completely hopeless."

Callie's laugh ended on a sob as she grabbed his hand. "Thanks, Rod. Just don't take him from me. Don't make him love you more than he loves me."

His heart ached for her. He caught the tear trembling on the edge of her lashes with his thumb and then cupped her face. "I don't think that's possible, sweetheart."

"Mom, Rod, I see a squirrel. Come look."

She grabbed a tissue and blew her nose. Through her watery smile, she said, "He called me *Mom*."

LONG AFTER DINNER, JESSE'S eyelids drooped as he recounted the wonders of the ranch to Linda, but he refused to slow down. Mostly, he talked about the wonders of Rod's ranch, since Price Is Right still needed a lot of work, and Callie didn't have one animal on her ranch except the wild kind.

Rod had put Jesse on a pony, and for a city kid, he was a natural. He could see why Callie had fallen hard for Jesse, besides their shared tragedy of a parent who had OD'd. The kid had a lot of spunk…just like Callie.

"You've had a long day, kiddo. I think it's time to hit the sack." Callie leaned over and brushed Jesse's dark hair out of his eyes.

"Just one more cookie, Mom. I promise I'll brush my teeth extrahard."

Callie smiled and pushed up from the sofa, heading for the plate of cookies on the kitchen counter.

"Your mom said time for bed. You can have another cookie tomorrow after dinner." Rod jumped from the sofa and grabbed Jesse, throwing him over his shoulder.

Jesse squealed as Callie shot Rod a glance through narrowed eyes. At least she couldn't accuse him of trying to win Jesse's affection with cookies.

Rod carried Jesse upstairs and deposited him in the bathroom next to his shiny new bedroom. Callie had followed them and stood with her shoulder propping up the bathroom doorjamb.

"I can handle it from here."

"I know you can." Rod pinched her chin and landed a kiss on her pursed lips.

He trotted downstairs and joined Linda, who had snapped open her laptop.

She peered at him over the top of her glasses. "This is a great environment for Jesse. Fresh air. Loving parents. Between you and me, the agency had some concerns about Callie and that studio in L.A. And when it burned down…" She shrugged and tapped a few more keys on her keyboard.

Who knows? Maybe Callie's marriage to him had given her more than the ranch. "I grew up in Silverhill. Can't beat it."

Callie jogged downstairs and peeked over Linda's shoulder. "A good report, I hope."

"I was just telling your husband, the setting is ideal for Jesse. And while we're more than happy to place a child with a loving single mother, having a father figure, especially for a boy like Jesse, is so valuable. I'll return to L.A. tomorrow with nothing but high praise for both of you. I'm sure this is going to work out now."

"Now?" Callie took a step backward. "You weren't sure before?"

A pink blush washed over Linda's face. "There was never any question about you, Callie. Jesse loves you and you love him. I'm just happy he has a father."

"Yeah, a husband and a father." Popping a piece of chocolate chip cookie into her mouth, Callie collected Jesse's cup and plate from the coffee table and dropped them into the sink.

"If you don't mind, I'm going to do a little reading in bed. I have to hop on another plane tomorrow." Linda excused herself and retreated upstairs to her guest bedroom.

Callie flopped down next to Rod and kicked her bare feet on top of the table. "Now that Linda's safely in her room, we don't have to make a big show out of sharing a bedroom tonight."

"I didn't think you had a problem when we shared a bedroom two nights ago." He ran a hand down her silky thigh and had the satisfaction of feeling a tremble roll through her body.

"That was before." She waved her arms around and bent her knee so his hand slid off her leg.

"Before I extricated you from that burning truck?"

She licked her lips. "Before I found out you were keeping a secret from me."

"Dana?" He stood up and stretched. "Even if I thought you were ready to hear that particular piece of news, it wasn't my secret to reveal."

She clasped her hands in her lap and drew her brows over her nose.

He had her there.

"Are you worried I'm keeping other secrets? Do you still believe I knew your identity when I married you?" He hunched over the table, his face inches from hers.

Releasing a long breath, she touched her forehead to his. "I'm afraid to believe in happily ever after. I'm afraid if I give in to you, you'll swallow me whole and spit me out."

He kissed her chocolate-flavored lips. "I may swallow you whole, Callie McClintock, but I'll never spit you out. You're way too sweet for that."

They reached for each other across the coffee table, fumbling, banging their knees, until Rod stepped over the table and crushed Callie to his chest.

Gasping, she hoisted herself up and wrapped her legs around his hips. A perfect fit.

He growled in her ear. "Now let's make sure Linda knows this is a marriage in every sense of the word."

With Callie still clinging to his body, Rod lurched toward the staircase, and then neatly swung her legs around and tucked her against his chest. He carried her into the bedroom they'd shared before, and the smell of dried rose petals and the citrus scent wafting from the adjoining bathroom made his mouth water and his groin tighten. Just like Pavlov's dog, his senses reacted to the memory of the last time he was in this room. Touching. Kissing. Tasting. Callie.

How had this woman—his wife—gotten under his skin so quickly and thoroughly?

She kneeled in front of him on the bed and yanked up his T-shirt. She pressed hot kisses from his chest to his belly, searing him, branding him.

They scrambled out of their clothes even faster than the previous time, and then Rod slowed things down, devouring every inch of her body with his hungry gaze as he straddled her. Callie crossed her arms behind her head, a lazy smile curving her lips, allowing him to drink his fill.

Nuzzling her ear, he whispered, "I'm not going to swallow you whole, but I am going to nibble my way across your body."

She wriggled beneath him, hooking her arms around his neck. "No spitting."

"Absolutely…Positively…No…Spitting." He separated each word with a kiss on a different part of her face, landing the last one on her mouth.

They reacquainted themselves with each other's needs and desires, and Rod felt as if he could never get enough of her. Was this how it felt to be in love? He wanted to imprint himself not only on her body, but on her soul.

LATER, CALLIE MOLDED HERSELF against his back, draping her leg over his hip. Her body, lush with languid satisfaction, felt soft and warm. He skimmed his hand down her thigh, and her content sighs stirred the hair at the nape of his neck, stirring his passion again.

He didn't give a damn about ranches or money or that deep pit of mistrust and abandonment that Callie had been filling with her love and laughter ever since the day he picked her up on the highway.

He wanted this woman forever.

Footsteps pounded down the hallway and a high-pitched cry made both of them bolt to a sitting position. The bedroom door burst open and Jesse barreled into the room, launching himself onto the bed.

"I saw a face at my window."

# Chapter Thirteen

Callie clutched the sheet to her throat as she put her other arm around Jesse's shaking shoulders. Rod had already yanked on his boxers and was scrambling from the bed. His feet slapped against the wood floor as he sprinted to Jesse's bedroom.

While Jesse buried his head in the covers, Callie grabbed Rod's T-shirt and pulled it over her head. Then she gathered Jesse in her arms and stroked his hair.

"It's all right now. Rod's going to take a look."

"Is everything okay?" Linda, struggling into a robe, appeared at the bedroom door and stepped inside.

"Jesse saw a face at his window." Callie swallowed. *Would Linda take Jesse away if she thought he was in an unsafe environment?*

The floorboards creaked and Callie held her breath until Rod appeared, filling the doorway with his imposing and comforting frame.

"I didn't see anything. The curtains are open and there's a tree branch right up against the screen."

Linda shook her head. "Jesse's been having some nightmares lately."

"He didn't have nightmares when he was with me before." Callie held Jesse tighter, threading her fingers through his curly, dark locks.

"They started after you left, Callie. I think he probably saw the shadow from the tree and imagined a face." She perched on the edge of the bed and rubbed Jesse's back. "Do you think that might be what happened, Jesse?"

He nodded, lifting his head from Callie's shoulder. "Can I stay with you and Rod tonight?"

Callie gazed across the top of Jesse's head into Rod's amused green eyes and shrugged.

"Sure." Rod chuckled. "Next time we'll close those curtains in your room."

"I left them open for a little light, since the moon is almost full. I'll get you a night-light instead, Jesse." Callie ruffled his hair.

Linda rose from the bed, her eyes avoiding Rod in all his masculine glory, still lounging against the doorjamb in his boxers. "I think we can all get back to sleep now."

Rod winked at Callie and stood aside for Linda. Then he closed the door and slid back into bed.

Jesse snuggled under the covers between them and drifted off to sleep almost immediately. Rod reached across Jesse's sleeping form and entwined his fingers with Callie's.

Callie whispered, "I think you embarrassed Linda by prancing around half naked."

"I was not prancing." He pulled her hand over and kissed her fingers. "At least she knows we're for real."

Callie melted a little around the edges and sighed. Could it get any freakin' better than this?

THE NEXT MORNING, ROD FINISHED a few more small jobs on Price Is Right and then returned to his own ranch to shower and change. When he was done, they drove Linda to the airport in Durango. She told Callie she'd be back for a surprise home visit in a month for the final evaluation. But Callie knew Rod had been a huge hit with Linda— even before she saw him in his boxers. In Rod, Callie had a valuable asset in her corner when it came to securing Jesse's adoption.

Twisting her hands behind her back, she glanced at him. Would he still be sharing her bed in a few months?

Rod's natural reserve took over after they dropped off Linda. Callie chatted with Jesse on the ride back, asking him to identify colors and shapes along the way. He was heading to kindergarten in the fall, and she wanted to give him a head start. The adoption agency figured Jesse's birth mother had done drugs while carrying Jesse, and some of his early development had been a little slow. Callie planned to make up for his disadvantaged start in life. At least her own mother had stayed clean during her pregnancy.

When Rod pulled up to the ranch, Callie said, "We're going to have some lunch, and then I think Jesse needs a nap. He had a little too much excitement last night."

"Can we go on the treasure hunt after?" Jesse's dark eyes shined with excitement. It was all he could talk about, after Callie told him about the treasure map.

"Sure."

"Can Rod come, too?" Jesse grabbed Rod's hat and put it on his head.

Callie laughed and shot a sideways glance at Rod. "Rod might be busy."

"I'll come along." Rod snatched his hat from Jesse's head. "But maybe I need to get you your own hat first."

"Black." Jesse crossed his arms. "I want a black cowboy hat."

"I'll see what I can do."

ROD PERCHED ON THE EDGE OF his chair and hardly touched his sandwich. After intercepting his hundredth meaningful glance over Jesse's head, Callie swept up the lunch dishes and deposited them in the sink. "Okay. Nap time. Then we'll hunt for treasure."

She read a quick story to Jesse, whose breathing deepened before she reached the end. She kissed his cheek and closed the curtains before returning downstairs.

Rod was flipping through a magazine and tossed it aside when Callie strode into the living room.

"What's up? Having second thoughts about being a father to Jesse? Because if so, we can call off the charade right—"

"Stop." He sliced his hand through the air. "I noticed something outside Jesse's bedroom window this morning when I was finishing some work out back."

Callie gulped, her throat suddenly dry. "What?"

"A broken branch and some threads from a sweater in the tree."

"You noticed all that from the ground?"

"I wasn't on the ground. I climbed the tree."

"You climbed the tree outside Jesse's bedroom window?"

"It's a perfect tree for climbing."

A pulse throbbed in Callie's temple. "Is that why you climbed it?"

"I climbed it because Jesse saw a face at his window last night."

Pain accompanied the throbbing, and Callie rubbed her head. "What made you do that?"

"Callie…" Rod placed his hands on her shoulders and they felt like lead weights. "Your father was in debt to a man who got murdered…in front of us. A structure on your property burned to the ground, and then we almost went over a cliff in my truck."

She shrugged away from him. "What does all that have to do with Jesse?"

"With Jesse? Nothing. But it's not inconceivable that someone was peering into my house through an open window to see what you were up to."

"The fire—nature's fury. The truck—an accident with your wheel." She gripped her upper arms and paced to the window.

"Maybe." He threw open the front door. "Do you want to see the evidence, or are you going to continue to hide your head like an ostrich, putting your life in danger— putting *Jesse's* life in danger?"

Spinning around, she cried, "I'd never do that."

"Not consciously, but maybe you're so anxious to have him here with you, you're dismissing these events too quickly."

Rod had a point. She hadn't wanted to examine any of those incidents too closely because she didn't want to delay her reunion with Jesse.

She blew out a breath. "Let's have a look."

She followed Rod to the back of the house, and he pointed to a large branch with leaves that tickled Jesse's window.

"Do you see the smaller branches to the right? They're drooping. Two of them were snapped…recently."

Callie squinted up at the tree that was still clinging to its canopy of green leaves, not yet willing to change color for fall. "A bird could've caused that."

"A pterodactyl?" Raising his brows, he laced his fingers together and crouched down. "I'll give you a boost so you can look for yourself. Then you can see the red threads on the upper branch."

Placing her hands on Rod's shoulders, Callie wedged her foot in his cupped hands. He hoisted her up, and she grasped the lowest branch. With another boost from Rod, Callie swung her leg over the branch and shimmied onto the tree.

She fingered the snapped twigs, tracing the white bark. This had happened recently.

Rod called from below. "Turn to your right. The threads are behind you."

Callie shifted her weight on the branch that afforded her a perfect view of Jesse's window, and cranked her head to the side. The rough bark had caught several threads of what appeared to be a red sweater.

Her knees trembled, and she leaned against the trunk for support. Why would somebody climb a tree and peer in the window at Jesse?

"Are you okay up there?"

She leaned forward, looking into Rod's face, that was lined with worry. "I'm fine, but you're right. Someone climbed this tree recently."

"I'll help you down." He spread his arms wide and Callie felt like falling into them and staying there forever.

Instead, she clambered over the branches until she sat on the lowest one, legs swinging below her. Rod reached for her waist and she slid into his arms.

Her face must've told him what she needed, because he crushed her against his chest. "Maybe we need to be more proactive about this. I'll contact Bobby's associates and tell them you have the money and are ready to turn it over."

She murmured against Rod's T-shirt. "I don't know how to contact Bobby's associates."

"Your father does."

"If they want their money, why would they be trying to kill me?"

"Who says they're trying to kill you? The fire occurred in an outlying structure, not the main house. The accident with the truck ended up being potentially deadly because of our location when the wheel came off. Otherwise, it would've been just another accident. And looking in a window doesn't constitute a deadly threat."

"Then what are they doing?"

"Maybe they're just trying to scare you into turning over the money."

"I'm ready and willing. All they have to do is ask."

"Call your father. Get this straightened out. You can't afford to have these people in your life, especially now that Jesse's here."

Callie bunched her hands into fists against Rod's back. "Do you think they'd hurt him?"

"Not while I'm here." He kissed the top of her head. "I'm moving in—permanently."

A tap at the window made Callie jump. She glanced up at Jesse, waving at her from his window. She smiled and waved back.

"I promised him a treasure hunt this afternoon, and that's what he's going to get."

FIFTEEN MINUTES LATER, after Jesse downed a glass of milk and munched through several slices of apple, the three of them perched on the front steps of her house at Price Is Right, Callie clutching the creased treasure map in her hand.

Jesse gripped a small, plastic shovel in his hand, while Rod retrieved a couple of grown-up shovels for himself and Callie. The map didn't specify if they'd need shovels to gain access to the treasure, or if they'd just have to move some rocks, but Callie wanted to be prepared and avoid disappointment for Jesse.

"Which direction?" Callie held the map in front of Jesse and pointed to the arrow facing right, and then to the compass rose her father had drawn in the lower right corner of the map.

Jesse shouted, "E!"

"That's right. East."

They trooped across the drive toward the fence bordering the eastern edge of the property. Rod had already repaired the wood slats that had rotted away or splintered.

He easily vaulted over the fence, while Callie squeezed through the middle slats and Jesse wriggled underneath.

Callie pointed out the landmarks on the property that her father had drawn onto the map, marveling at the detail. What had happened to her father, to change him from the careful boy who had created this map to the ramshackle man who couldn't return her phone calls?

Jesse squealed and scampered from rock to rock, jumping back and forth over the little creek that zigzagged through the property.

A sense of contentment infused Callie's bones when Rod swung Jesse onto his shoulders, bouncing him up and down.

"Look, Mom. I'm tall."

"Can you spy two trees next to each other, with a hammock between them?"

Jesse shielded his eyes as if gazing across the ocean from the deck of a ship. "What's a hammock?"

"It's like a swing."

"I see it! I see it!"

"Okay. We're almost at our destination. What kind of treasure do you think we'll find?"

"Gold money." Jesse waved his arms wildly.

Rod chimed in. "Rubies, emeralds and diamonds."

*Not likely.* Callie snorted to herself. Even if her father had ever buried anything of value, he'd have claimed it long ago and gambled it away.

Rod and Jesse entered into a very male game of one-upmanship, trying to outdo each other in naming the riches they'd find until Jesse blurted out, "Cracker Jacks."

"Silly." Callie plucked a wildflower and tickled Jesse's cheek with it.

Rod lifted a giggling and squirming Jesse off his shoulders and handed him the plastic shovel. "Where to next?"

Squinting at the map, Callie traced the dotted line from the hammock to a pile of rocks. She had to hand it to Dad—he had impressive artistic skills as a child. She'd always assumed she'd inherited her artistic talent from her mom, who'd fancied herself an artist—when she wasn't stoned.

She looked up and spotted a cluster of four boulders beyond the two trees. "I think X marks the spot right over there. The map shows one of those rocks rolling forward."

"Let the men handle this." Rod strode forward with the shovel over his shoulder, and Jesse traipsed behind him, his shovel over the same shoulder.

"What do you think, Jesse?" Rod nudged the rock with the toe of his boot. "Can you help me move this?"

The two of them crouched down and rolled the rock forward, revealing a semicircle of cleared earth bordered by the other three boulders.

"I hope no one beat us to the treasure. This looks like fresh dirt." Rod glanced over his shoulder at Callie, his brow creased.

She sat on one of the rocks and stirred the dirt with her

foot. "Maybe it just looks different because it's beneath this rock, moister—darker."

"We'll see. Let's get started." Rod plunged the tip of his shovel into the ground and scooped out a clump of earth.

Jesse followed with his plastic shovel and Callie drove hers into the hole they started. They continued in a rhythmic pattern, Jesse throwing more dirt back into the hole than out of it.

After several minutes, Callie's shovel clanged as it hit metal. The contact reverberated up to her hands and she dropped the shovel, more out of surprise than pain. She couldn't believe her father had followed through with anything like this.

Jesse danced around at the edge of the hole. "We found it! We found it!"

Rod scraped the dirt off the object, and dug around it—until a rusted metal box appeared. Brushing it off, he lifted the box out of the hole and placed it on the boulder next to Callie. He flicked the broken lock hanging from the latch. "At least we won't need a key to open it."

"Jesse, do you want to do the honors?" Rod spun to shove a box toward Jesse.

"No." Callie snatched the metal box from the rock and hugged it to her chest against her hammering heart.

Jesse's dark eyes widened and Rod lifted one brow. "Do you think there might be spiders in there? Scorpions maybe?"

Jesse's eyes took up half his face.

Callie rubbed the rough edge of the container with the pad of her thumb. She didn't know what she thought. A finger of cold fear had traced a line down her spine when Rod pulled the box from its hiding place.

"I—I don't know." She loosened her grip on the treasure

box and placed it back on the rock. *Don't be ridiculous.* What did she expect to be in the box, a head? It wasn't nearly big enough.

Rod grabbed the latch and lifted the lid smoothly. Too smoothly for something buried for almost fifty years.

The metal lid banged back against the rock and Callie jumped, gasping. Leaning over, she peered into the box.

Choking back a cry, she covered her mouth and turned her eyes, almost as big as Jesse's, toward Rod.

# Chapter Fourteen

"That's not gold money." Jesse's disgusted voice broke the silence hanging over the little group. "Can I swing on the hammock now?"

Without taking her eyes off the contents of the box, Callie nodded.

Rod called after Jesse's scampering form. "Be careful. It might break."

"What's a tape doing in here?" Callie reached forward and pinched the minicassette tape between two fingers.

"Your father."

"That's what he was doing in Silverhill. He came back here to bury this tape in his secret hiding place. He's the one who left the veil at the house that first night." Her lips stuck to her teeth as she tried to form her next words. "Do you think this is what Bobby was looking for when he searched the house?"

"Yep."

Rod shuffled through the remaining contents of the box—a few feathers, an arrowhead, a calcified bird's egg—treasures for a young boy. Betrayal, subterfuge for the adult man.

She licked her lips. "What do you think it is?"

"Something Bobby wanted back."

"Something his killer wants even more?"

Jesse yelped and they both swung around. He dangled in a tangled heap from the hammock, which had twisted around his small body. Rod's loud laugh boomed, loosening the knot of fear in Callie's belly.

She had to get her dad on the phone…now. While Rod charged over to rescue Jesse, Callie dug her cell phone out of the pocket of her shorts and selected Dad's number from her short list of contacts.

When she got his voice mail, she almost shouted into the phone. "I found the tape in your little hiding place. What is it and who wants it? And you'd better call me back this time. I know all your dirty little secrets and I'll make your life a living hell if you don't."

She snapped the phone shut and, clutching the metal box under her arm, joined Rod and Jesse untangling the hammock. As she helped them, she whispered to Rod. "Do you have a minicassette recorder around your house?"

"I don't, but I'll bet Dana and Rafe have one. Comes in handy in their line of work." He hoisted Jesse back into the center of the hammock and gave him a push.

"Is Dana still in town?"

"Yeah. Do you want to try that dinner again—tonight?"

Callie's cell phone buzzed and she held up her index finger to Rod. Glancing at the display, she exhaled. Finally. Obviously the threat worked. "What's going on, Dad? Why'd you bury a tape on the ranch?"

He chuckled. "It's a good spot, isn't it? How'd you find it?"

"Grandpa Ennis kept that treasure map you made in a safe deposit box. I figured it would be something fun for Jesse to do. Imagine my surprise."

"My father kept that map? I'll be damned."

"You're right. You will be if you don't tell me what this is all about."

Rod kept swinging Jesse in the hammock and answering a thousand questions from him, but his expression told Callie he was intent on her one-sided conversation.

"I don't know what's on the tape, Callie. I took it from Bobby, but I have no idea what it is or why it's so important to him."

"Why'd you steal it then?"

"Insurance. You ran out on the wedding, taking with you any chance I had of paying back Bobby. Knowing the tape was important to Bobby, I filched it to use as leverage. I came out to the old homestead and hid it, to wait for the right moment. Then you got married and agreed to pay my debt, and I didn't need the tape."

Callie pressed her hand against her forehead. "Did Bobby realize you'd stolen the tape?"

"Probably. But what does it matter now? Bobby's dead."

"It matters…" She waved at Jesse and then turned her back on him. "It matters because someone murdered Bobby, and maybe that someone wants the tape, too."

Dad cleared his throat. "What makes you think that?"

Callie closed her eyes as images of the fire and the car crash danced across her lids. "Just some weird stuff going on."

He scoffed. "That's your imagination."

"Did you know Bobby was interested in branching out into dealing drugs?"

Her father sucked in a sharp breath. "I didn't, but it doesn't surprise me. He had a lot of irons in the fire."

"Well, thanks a bunch for putting me in danger." Callie

scuffed the toe of her sneaker into the dirt. "Did you know you might have another daughter here in Silverhill?"

"There's always that possibility. Why are you laying all this on me now, Callie? I called you back. I told you everything I know. Isn't that enough?"

"I guess it is for you, Dad. You never could give very much, could you?"

Before he could answer, Callie ended the call and spun around toward Jesse and Rod, pasting a smile on her face. "I think we should clean up before we meet Rafe and Dana for dinner."

Callie had no intention of keeping Jesse away from *his* family.

Rod made good on his promise to move in with Callie, hauling some clothes and other items to her place before dinner. After discovering that minicassette, his promise took on a whole new urgency.

Jonah could've at least warned Callie that he'd buried some evidence against Bobby on the property. Of course, as Rod had pointed out to Callie, her father hadn't known at the time that she'd make her way to the ranch after her escape from marital bliss.

But she'd argued back that he had an opportunity to tell her when she called to let him know she was married and had taken up residence on the ranch. And she was right.

Once Callie had decided to give up on her rose-colored dreams of having some kind of normal relationship with her dirt-bag father, she'd shown an awesome ferocity.

He'd have to watch himself.

He hung up the last of his shirts and closed the lid of his suitcase. "Where should I put this?"

Callie, her legs crossed beneath her on the bed, frowned

and asked for about the hundredth time, "What's on that tape?"

He sank next to her on the bed, draping an arm across her shoulders. "We'll find out in less than an hour, and we'll have a cop and an FBI agent there to handle any fallout."

"I think it has something to do with Bobby's plan to intercept that drug shipment." She shivered beneath his arm. "But why would the drug dealer think we had the tape, or know anything about it?"

"No point in speculating. We'll find out soon enough." He squeezed her stiff shoulder, wanting to make this all disappear for her. "Is Jesse ready?"

"Yeah, I made him take a bath, much to his disgust." She caught his hand and put her soft lips against his palm. "Thanks for entertaining him while I was on the phone with my dad."

"I had fun."

"For an uptight cowboy who has to listen to classical music to unwind, you've adapted amazingly well to an instant family. When you took me on, you didn't realize you'd get a son in the bargain."

He swept aside her hair and brushed a kiss against the back of her neck. "And what a bargain I got."

He was just about to tumble across the bed, with her in his arms, when Jesse popped his head into the room. "I made a spaceship."

AFTER THEY INSPECTED JESSE'S Lego spaceship, they piled into Rod's car and drove to Rafe's house. Callie bounced her leg and punched the buttons on the radio on the ride over. Rod knew she'd want to listen to the tape as soon as they walked in the door.

When they pulled into the driveway, his niece, Kelsey,

skipped down the front steps and hugged him around the waist. She laced her fingers behind her back as she watched Callie help Jesse from the car.

Then Callie turned and held her arms wide and Kelsey hugged her, too. Kelsey whispered, "Sorry—" but Callie put a finger to her lips.

She introduced Kelsey to Jesse, and Kelsey took him by the hand to lead him into the house. Rafe and Dana then crowded the door and Dana extended a tentative hand to Callie.

"I'm sorry I overreacted." Callie grasped the proffered hand. "I'd be thrilled to contribute some DNA for a test."

Dana pulled her forward and kissed her cheek. "You did not overreact. I'm sure it was a shock. We all wanted to break it to you more gently, but our daughter is kind of impulsive."

"Sometimes that's a good thing." She tilted her chin toward Kelsey and Jesse, on the floor, thumbing through books.

"Do you have that tape?" Rafe poked Rod in the ribs. "After you called this afternoon, I brought home the mini-cassette player from the station."

Callie shifted her gaze toward the kids on the floor. "We have no idea what's on that tape."

"Kelsey." Dana tapped her daughter on the shoulder. "I'm going to get you and Jesse a couple of glasses of lemonade. You can take the books out back, but stay on the deck."

As Dana led the two of them into the kitchen, Rafe stuffed his hands in his pockets. "I'm hoping this tape gives me some information about Bobby's killer. We have nothing. And the FBI hasn't been much help. His murder was a professional hit, or at least a practiced one."

"I'm hoping the tape gives Callie some peace of mind. We think someone climbed a tree to look into her house the other night." Rod plucked the tape out of the front pocket of his shirt and dropped it into Rafe's hand.

Rafe formed a fist around it. "And the accident with your truck?"

"Do you think that's related to all this?" Callie took a step closer to Rod, and he tucked an arm around her waist and pulled her snug against his body.

Rafe snorted. "I know my brother, and to say he's compulsive about his vehicles—well, about *everything*—is an understatement. No way he had loose lug nuts on the wheel of his truck."

The kids emerged from the kitchen, clutching glasses tinkling with ice in pale yellow lemonade. Dana gathered their books and opened the sliding glass door to the back deck. She left the door open and slid the screen shut behind her. "Where's the tape recorder, babe?"

"In my bag." Rafe pointed to a black, soft-sided briefcase in the entryway.

Dana bit her lip as she clawed through the bag. "If only you were half as compulsive as your brother."

"Then I'd be my other brother, Ryder." Rafe winked at Callie, and Rod silently thanked him for his lighthearted attitude as Callie laughed.

"Found it." Dana pulled out a small device that fit into the palm of her hand. She flipped it over. "Does it have fresh batteries?"

"I put some in at the station."

"You continually amaze me." She handed the cassette player to Rod.

He clicked open the receptacle for the tape and Rafe slid it in. Rod punched the Play button and held his breath.

The tape emitted some scratchy sounds, and then a

man's smooth voice said, "Hey, Nicky. It's Bobby. I have our prey in my snare. He's into me for some big bucks."

Rod's brain raced as Callie clutched his hand. Bobby set out to entrap Jonah Price.

A man's voice responded. "Yo, Bobby. You're on speaker. Nicky's in the room. How much you got him for?"

"Over a hundred grand."

"Has he called the daughter yet?"

Callie gasped, and Rod rested a steadying hand on the small of her back.

Rafe voiced what they were all thinking. "This was some kind of setup."

Rafe rewound the tape to replay Bobby's response to the question.

"That's why I'm calling. She's here in Las Cruces."

The screen door slid open and they all jumped.

Kelsey held out an empty glass. "Jesse wants more lemonade. Watcha listening to?"

"Grownup stuff." Dana waved her hand toward the kitchen. "Pour him another glass and don't spill."

Rafe had stopped the tape, his finger hovering over the button. "On the orders of this Nicky, Bobby ensnared your father into a large debt to him, to lure you out to New Mexico. Maybe the whole thing was planned from the beginning, to get the ranch and the money."

"How would Bobby or this drug dealer, Nicky, know about the ranch? Seems like a convoluted and risky way to get your hands on some money." Callie tucked her hair behind one ear and leaned her head against Rod's shoulder.

The muscles in Rod's neck formed hard knots, and pain shot up the back of his skull. He didn't like this. Was the fire at Callie's studio in L.A. part of this same plan? What did they want with Callie?

Finally, Kelsey floated out of the kitchen, carefully holding a full glass of lemonade, and slid onto the deck.

Rafe punched the button.

"Do you think you can pull this off without screwing up?" a woman's voice growled over the tape, and Rod whistled. A female drug dealer.

Bobby chuckled. "I'll mess up this chick so bad, no social worker in her right mind would let her adopt a kid."

Callie sagged against Rod, and he tightened his arm around her.

The woman's voice continued, as sultry as a ribbon of dark chocolate. "You get this right, Papi, and I'll let you in on my next big score. Maybe I'll even let you back in my bed."

"When is the next big score, Nicky?"

Nicky clicked her tongue. "Don't get greedy. All in good time. We'll talk once I take my son, Jesse, back from that bitch Callie Price."

The pain that had been creeping up Rod's skull hit him like a sledgehammer as Callie cried out.

"Go back, go back." Callie tore the cassette player out of Rafe's hands. "I know that voice."

But the woman's voice on the tape was drowned out when Kelsey tripped into the room, panting, her face white.

"I—I can't find Jesse."

## Chapter Fifteen

A sheet of ice crawled across Callie's flesh, and she dropped the cassette player from her stiff fingers. Rod stepped behind her, breaking her fall as she stumbled backward.

Rafe immediately retrieved his weapon from a safe in the closet and charged outside. Dana rushed to her daughter and gripped her shoulders. "Where did you leave him?"

"On the deck." Tears pooled in Kelsey's eyes. "I told him to stay on the deck while I came in to get his lemonade. When I got back outside, he was gone. I thought he just went into the backyard, but he's not there. I looked."

Rod chafed Callie's hands as he led her to the sofa. "I'm going to help Rafe. Dana, look after her."

Callie broke away from him, a flame of rage curling through her body, giving her life. "I'm coming with you. I know who has Jesse. I recognized her voice on the tape. It's Amber Lewis."

Rod's jaw dropped.

Dana gasped. "Amber Lewis, the house hunter, is Nicky Torres, the drug dealer?"

Callie's galloping heart skipped a few more beats. "Nicky Torres?"

"I didn't say anything when the tape was playing, but

when I heard the woman's voice and Bobby calling her Nicky, I knew it was Nicky Torres. She's a big-time drug dealer in the Southwest."

"You didn't notice a big-time drug dealer traipsing around Silverhill this past week, pretending to look for a winter home?" Rod folded his arms over his chest, bunching his fists against his biceps.

"I haven't worked a drug case in the Indian Country Crimes Unit involving Torres yet. I've never seen her picture, just heard the name around the Bureau office." Dana wound Kelsey's ponytail around her hand. "I'm dropping Kelsey off with my great-aunt, and then I'm coming with you."

"Where are you all going?" Rafe strode into the room, picking off twigs and bits of leaves from his shirt.

Dana gave her daughter a little push. "Go to your room and pack for overnight." When Kelsey disappeared down the hallway, Dana turned to Rafe. "We've identified Jesse's kidnapper. She's a drug dealer named Nicky Torres. She's Jesse's biological mother, and she's been posing as a house-hunting tourist here in Silverhill for the past week."

Rafe cursed and dragged his hands through his hair. "Isn't she staying at Gracie's place?"

"She was, but she won't be there for long now." Rod grabbed Callie's hand, pulling her toward the front door.

Leaving Dana behind with Kelsey, Rod, Rafe and Callie ran to Rod's rental car. As he squeezed into the backseat, Rafe pulled out his cell phone. Callie twisted around in her seat. "Who are you calling?"

"I'm going to get my deputy, Brice Kellogg, out there."

"Not with sirens wailing and gun drawn, I hope." Rod cranked on the engine and peeled out of the driveway.

"Amber—Nicky probably doesn't realize we know her identity."

Rafe tapped his phone against his chin. "Probably not, unless she's aware of the tape and knows Callie found it. But she just kidnapped a child. She's not going to be hanging around, shooting the breeze with Gracie."

"I just don't want her to panic and harm Jesse." Callie clenched her fists, digging her nails into her palms. "She left him in a trash bin when he was a baby, so I know she's capable of anything. What does she want with him now?"

"She probably killed Bobby, too." Rod clutched the steering wheel as he made a sharp turn onto the highway.

"Probably, and I'd like to know why. It can't be that tape. A voice taped from a telephone conversation isn't very effective or incriminating evidence, even if Bobby Jingo was stupid enough to believe it was." Rafe got Brice on the phone and told him to stake out Gracie's place on foot, without alerting the guests.

As they rounded the bend to the stretch of highway leading to Gracie Malone's bed-and-breakfast, Callie dug her nails into Rod's forearm. "There's a car in the driveway with the trunk open. It must be hers. Let me do this."

Rod cut the headlights and eased the car into a pull-out at the side of the highway.

"Do what?" Rafe had pulled his weapon from its holster as he hunched forward between the front seats.

"After taking Jesse, she returned to her hotel. She doesn't realize we know Amber Lewis is Nicky Torres and Nicky Torres is Jesse's biological mother. Maybe I can still get close enough to rescue Jesse."

"She's not going to parade Jesse out of the B and B in

front of you, and then blithely drive off with your son."
Rod shut down the engine and slumped in his seat. "Let's
wait here until Brice contacts Rafe. The three of us will
go in together, while you wait in the car."

Callie twisted her hands in her lap. If Rod thought she
was going to stay put in the car while some drug dealer
absconded with Jesse, he had a thing or two to learn about
his new bride.

Maybe she could appeal to Nicky woman-to-woman,
mom-to-mom. If the three men rushed in with their guns
blazing, what would Nicky do to Jesse? She might just
hold a gun to his head while the three cowboys surrounded
her with their helpless weapons.

Nope. She was Jesse's mother, and just like a lioness,
her claws were out and her teeth sharpened.

As Rod and Rafe discussed their plan, waiting for Brice
to call—waiting for Nicky to get Jesse into that car—
Callie slid off her seat belt. She inched her fingers to the
car door handle and gripped it. Rafe's phone rang, and
Callie yanked the handle and stumbled from the car, pulling the door closed behind her so Nicky wouldn't notice
the dome light.

A window buzzed down behind her and Rod hissed,
"Callie!"

She took long strides toward the B and B, knowing Rod
wouldn't dare start up the car and come after her. They
didn't want Nicky to know they were there.

As Callie edged around to the side of the property, she
noticed Nicky had closed the trunk of her Mercedes, leaving the keys dangling from the lock. When had she done
that? Had she noticed Rod's car parked down the road.
Callie twisted around and could see no sign of Rod's car
in the pull-out.

She crept along the path to the back cottage and drew

up sharply when the door swung open, spilling light on the gravel. Nicky appeared in the doorway, stuffing a pair of sneakers into a shoulder bag. She must've worn those to hike through the canyon behind Rafe and Dana's house, to snatch Jesse. How long had she been following her? Spying on her?

Callie stepped into the light.

Nicky snapped up the handle of a suitcase and turned, nearly tripping over her feet when she spotted Callie.

"Callie, what are you doing here? I don't have time to visit. I'm leaving tonight, but I'll be back to touch base with my Realtor."

Callie swallowed and peered behind Nicky, and then turned to check the car, the driver-side door open, the inside light glowing. If Nicky had Jesse, where was he? Maybe she ordered some minion to snatch him. The thought caused a sour lump of fear to lodge in her belly.

Callie's brain whirred. If she didn't tell Nicky now that Jesse was missing, Nicky would realize that Callie suspected her. If she did tell her, Nicky would wonder what the hell she was doing here, with her kid missing.

The bright friendliness of Nicky's voice darkened to a low murmur. "Looking for something, Callie?"

Nicky knew.

Callie dug her heels into the gravel and clenched her jaw. Narrowing her eyes, she hissed back, "You know it, bitch. Where's my son?"

Smoky laughter escaped from Nicky's lips. "Jesse's mine."

"You threw him away. Literally. Now he's mine."

Shrugging one shoulder, Nicky reached into her purse and withdrew a gun. "Circumstances got in the way. After I left Jesse, I did some time for drugs. When I got out, I tried to get him back legally, but those people wouldn't give him to me. Then you showed up."

Callie kept her gaze trained on Nicky's face, away from the weapon pointed at her chest. "The fire at my studio?"

"I knew the adoption agency wouldn't leave Jesse with you without a place to live. How'd you find out about me? I saw it in your face the moment you showed up here."

"Bobby had a tape of a phone conversation. I recognized your voice. My father stole that tape, and I found it."

"Bobby." The gun wavered for a moment. "Did you sleep with him before you discovered he was a two-bit criminal?"

The hard edge of Nicky's voice slipped. Did she really care about Bobby?

Callie twisted her lips into a smile. "Yeah, I did. Well, you know how persuasive he can be."

Nicky choked. "Bitch."

She *did* care.

"Is that why you killed him?" Callie snapped her fingers. "I get it. Bobby was just supposed to make my life a living hell, so the agency would never give Jesse back to me. Instead, he decided to marry me, take my money and use it to double-cross you."

"Let's just say he overstepped his duties."

"I guess you just weren't that good."

"Good enough to take Jesse from you." Nicky waved the gun. "Now get out of my way."

Where could Jesse be? Callie's gaze flicked to the closed trunk and back to Nicky's suitcase. Why had she closed the trunk of her car when she still had a suitcase to load?

A twig snapped in the underbrush and Callie caught her

breath. Was that Brice? Her eyes shifted back to Nicky, impatiently tapping her toe.

Callie took a steadying breath. "Where's Jesse?"

"Get out of my way or I'll shoot you where you stand. I almost got you when I took out Bobby. Should've done it, but then I would've had to go back to L.A. to collect Jesse. This way, that stupid agency brought him *to* me."

*Keep her talking....*

Sliding her hands into her back pockets, Callie asked, "Were you responsible for the fire at the ranch, and Rod's truck, too?"

"Just trying to screw up your life so the social worker would realize what a mess you were. I guess you tricked her into believing your marriage to that long drink of cowboy was for real, huh?"

"Jesse loves me and I love him. There's nothing you could've done to change that. There's nothing you can do now."

Nicky snorted. "I've already done it. You'll never see my son again."

The gravel crunched beneath Nicky's high-heeled boots as she made a move toward the car. Callie couldn't allow her anywhere near the trunk. She couldn't allow her to take off in that car. Rafe and Brice wouldn't be able to run her off the road or shoot at the car with Jesse in the trunk.

"How about you open the trunk and let me see Jesse now." Callie stepped between the car and Nicky, whose dark eyes widened, and raised her voice so the person in the bushes could hear. "The keys are already in the trunk. Open it."

"I'm the one with the gun. Step aside." Nicky hitched her bag higher on her shoulder and wobbled on her high heels.

In a flash, a figured darted out of the bushes. Rod yelled, "Duck, Callie."

In a single movement, Callie crouched and charged toward Nicky's legs. The blast of the gun exploded over her head and she heard the ping of a bullet against chrome.

Callie missed her target and hit the dirt, but Rod had tackled Nicky and was struggling to wrestle the gun from her hand.

Rod could handle that skinny witch.

As Rafe and Brice charged the scene, Callie scrambled to the Mercedes and wrenched the key in the lock of the trunk. It lifted and the side lights illuminated Jesse, his body curled in a fetal position.

With stiff fingers, Callie felt for his pulse and almost fainted with relief. She gathered his sleeping form in her arms, just as a single shot from the gun rang out.

Clasping Jesse to her chest, Callie turned to find Rafe and Brice, guns drawn and pointed toward the couple on the ground.

Nicky was sprawled beneath Rod, a knife clutched in her hand. As a trickle of blood soaked into the gravel, Nicky's fingers opened and a knife slid from her hand.

Callie's heart thundered beneath the weight of Jesse's body and her mouth felt like sandpaper. *Please, not Rod!* Not her husband.

Then Rod rolled to his side and struggled to his knees. "She was going to throw the knife at Callie. I had to shoot her."

# *Epilogue*

Callie's bare feet sank into the soft rose petals that littered the path to the arbor that was entwined with flowers, where her husband waited for her.

Half the town of Silverhill had gathered at Price Is Right for her second wedding to Rod. Rod's two best men, his brothers Ryder and Rafe, stood by his side, while Callie's maid of honor, her sister Dana, preceded her down the aisle.

Dad couldn't make it.

Her tea-length wedding dress brushed her calves as Rod took her hand and pulled her next to him. They recited their vows, hers a love poem to the man who rescued her in every way, his short, real, from the heart.

When Rod slipped the gold band on her finger on top of the cheap gemstone he'd bought in Vegas, Callie felt as if they'd come full circle.

When he kissed her lips and whispered, "I love you," she felt as if she'd floated to heaven.

Several hours later, after all the guests had left, Callie bumped her hip against the screen door, clutching two sodas in her hands and one against her chest. She handed the sodas to Dana and Ryder's wife, Julia, just as Rod and his brothers secured the last bolt into the play set. Then

Kelsey corralled her two young cousins, Jesse and Shelby, and they all scampered toward the swings.

Jesse squealed, "Push me, Kelsey."

"She's good with him." Callie hopped up on the newly installed railing around the porch, hooking her foot on the side post.

"She still feels guilty about the night Nicky snatched him from our backyard." Dana popped the lid of the can and the soda fizzled around the rim. "It doesn't look like he has any ill effects from the chloroform that Nicky used on him."

"He vomited when he woke up and slept a lot those first few days, but he's fine now." Rod's cell phone buzzed in her pocket, and Callie checked the display. Unknown number.

"He's been through a lot. And so have you." Dana placed her hand on Callie's arm. "Are you okay with everything?"

"You mean the fact that you're my half sister? I already told you, Dana. I'm thrilled." She hugged Dana stiffly. Familial affection didn't come naturally to her, but she wanted to try with Dana.

Dana patted her back. "I am, too. Have you told…our father yet?"

"I told him. He wasn't too surprised. He remembers your mom well."

Dana raised her brows and Callie grabbed her hand and squeezed, a more genuine response this time. "Don't bother trying to win his affection, Dana. You'll never get it."

"Getting to know my sister is good enough for me."

A flood of warmth coursed through Callie's veins. She didn't have to try hard to win Dana's affection. Her gaze wandered to Rod, doubled over with laughter at something

Rafe said, and then tracked over to Jesse, giggling as his cousin pushed him higher and higher in the swing.

At the same moment, Rod straightened up and blew her a kiss and Jesse screamed, "Mom, Mom, look at me."

Heck, she didn't have to do a thing to win their love.

The men joined them on the porch, complaining that they didn't have anything to drink.

"We're the ones who did all the work." Ryder hung over the back of Julia's chair and kissed the top of her head before snatching the can from her hand.

She slapped his hand, while her other caressed her pregnant belly. "I think Rod and Rafe did all the work. You supervised."

Rod slipped his arm around Callie, and she handed him her soda. He gestured toward Dana. "So, did you get some credit from the Bureau for taking down Nicky Torres?"

"Technically, *you* took down Nicky Torres, but yeah, everyone had big smiles on their faces when I went up to Denver."

Rafe grabbed his wife's soda and took a long swig and wiped his brow. "Did you ever figure out if Nicky knew about Bobby's tape?"

"She didn't know about it and didn't really care about it. At least that's what she told me when she had me at gunpoint." Callie tilted her head. "Funny enough, I think she cared about Bobby. He made her angry when he didn't take care of me like he promised, and instead tried to marry me to get my money to double-cross her. Once the adoption agency did a background check on Bobby, they never would've handed Jesse over to me. So, in a way, he was doing his job, but he tried to screw Nicky at the same time."

"Bobby was strictly small potatoes. I don't know how he got mixed up with a big-time drug dealer like Nicky

Torres, but even an amateur should've known not to mess with her." Rafe patted Callie's knee. "So you solved my crime, too."

Julia waved at Shelby, who had climbed to the top of the slide. "Does Jesse remember anything about the kidnapping?"

"He remembers falling. I think Nicky must've snatched him from behind when Kelsey went into the house and then put the chloroform-soaked cloth over his nose and mouth. I told him he fell outside and hit his head."

"Kelsey is so relieved we found him. She blamed herself." Dana drew her dark brows over her nose and bit her lip.

Callie shook her head. "It wasn't Kelsey's fault. We never told her Jesse was in danger. I refused to believe he was in danger."

Dana dropped her voice to a whisper. "Kelsey has that whole ESP thing going on, just like I do. It's a dubious gift from her Ute heritage. She thought she should've *known* Jesse was in danger, but it doesn't always work that way."

Callie's eyes widened. She could tell her new family was going to be a source of continual surprises.

Rod's phone buzzed in her pocket again, and she pulled it out. "You have a voice mail. The phone rang before, but a number, not a name, flashed on the display."

She dropped the phone in his open palm, and the rest of them continued to chatter, everyone trying to talk over each other at once. Callie joined in the conversation, navigating her first big family free-for-all with a smile on her face.

Rod snapped his phone shut, scowling as he tucked it in his shirt pocket. Callie's heart skipped a beat and she ran her hand along his thigh. "Anything wrong?"

Shrugging broad shoulders that could carry the weight of the world, Rod took another gulp of soda. "That was Rio McClintock, our half brother. He's coming for a visit."

Silence descended on the group for just a moment, before a cacophony of voices erupted again.

Callie kissed the frown from between Rod's eyes. Yep, a family full of surprises. But *her* family.

\* \* \* \* \*

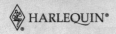

# INTRIGUE®

## COMING NEXT MONTH

### Available October 12, 2010

# *LARGER-PRINT BOOKS!*

## *GET 2 FREE LARGER-PRINT NOVELS*

## *PLUS 2 FREE GIFTS!*

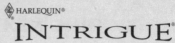

**HARLEQUIN®**

# INTRIGUE®

### Breathtaking Romantic Suspense

**YES!** Please send me 2 FREE LARGER-PRINT Harlequin Intrigue® novels and my 2 FREE gifts (gifts are worth about $10). After receiving them, if I don't wish to receive any more books, I can return the shipping statement marked "cancel." If I don't cancel, I will receive 6 brand-new novels every month and be billed just $4.99 per book in the U.S. or $5.74 per book in Canada. That's a saving of at least 13% off the cover price! It's quite a bargain! Shipping and handling is just 50¢ per book.* I understand that accepting the 2 free books and gifts places me under no obligation to buy anything. I can always return a shipment and cancel at any time. Even if I never buy another book from Harlequin, the two free books and gifts are mine to keep forever.

199/399 HDN E5MS

Name          (PLEASE PRINT)

Address          Apt. #

City          State/Prov.          Zip/Postal Code

Signature (if under 18, a parent or guardian must sign)

Mail to the **Harlequin Reader Service:**
**IN U.S.A.:** P.O. Box 1867, Buffalo, NY 14240-1867
**IN CANADA:** P.O. Box 609, Fort Erie, Ontario L2A 5X3

Not valid for current subscribers to Harlequin Intrigue Larger-Print books.

**Are you a subscriber to Harlequin Intrigue books and want to receive the larger-print edition? Call 1-800-873-8635 today!**

* Terms and prices subject to change without notice. Prices do not include applicable taxes. N.Y. residents add applicable sales tax. Canadian residents will be charged applicable provincial taxes and GST. Offer not valid in Quebec. This offer is limited to one order per household. All orders subject to approval. Credit or debit balances in a customer's account(s) may be offset by any other outstanding balance owed by or to the customer. Please allow 4 to 6 weeks for delivery. Offer available while quantities last.

**Your Privacy:** Harlequin Books is committed to protecting your privacy. Our Privacy Policy is available online at www.eHarlequin.com or upon request from the Reader Service. From time to time we make our lists of customers available to reputable third parties who may have a product or service of interest to you. If you would prefer we not share your name and address, please check here. ☐

**Help us get it right**—We strive for accurate, respectful and relevant communications. To clarify or modify your communication preferences, visit us at www.ReaderService.com/consumerschoice.

# HARLEQUIN®

## A Romance

# FOR EVERY MOOD™

Spotlight on

## Inspirational

Wholesome romances
that touch the heart and soul.

See the next page
to enjoy a sneak peek from
the Love Inspired® inspirational series.

*See below for a sneak peek at
our inspirational line, Love Inspired®.
Introducing HIS HOLIDAY BRIDE
by bestselling author Jillian Hart*

Autumn Granger gave her horse rein to slide toward the town's new sheriff.

"Hey, there." The man in a brand-new Stetson, black T-shirt, jeans and riding boots held up a hand in greeting. He stepped away from his four-wheel drive with "Sheriff" in black on the doors and waded through the grasses. "I'm new around here."

"I'm Autumn Granger."

"Nice to meet you, Miss Granger. I'm Ford Sherman, from Chicago." He knuckled back his hat, revealing the most handsome face she'd ever seen. Big blue eyes contrasted with his sun-tanned complexion.

"I'm guessing you haven't seen much open land. Out here, you've got to keep an eye on cows or they're going to tear your vehicle apart."

"What?" He whipped around. Sure enough, mammoth black-and-white creatures had started to gnaw on his four-wheel drive. They clustered like a mob, mouths and tongues and teeth bent on destruction. One cow tried to pry the wiper off the windshield, another chewed on the side mirror. Several leaned through the open window, licking the seats.

"Move along, little dogie." He didn't know the first thing about cattle.

The entire herd swiveled their heads to study him curiously. Not a single hoof shifted. The animals soon returned to chewing, licking, digging through his possessions.

Autumn laughed, a warm and wonderful sound. "Thanks,

I needed that." She then pulled a bag from behind her saddle and waved it at the cows. "Look what I have, guys. Cookies."

Cows swung in her direction, and dozens of liquid brown eyes brightened with cookie hopes. As she circled the car, the cattle bounded after her. The earth shook with the force of their powerful hooves.

"Next time, you're on your own, city boy." She tipped her hat. The cowgirl stayed on his mind, the sweetest thing he had ever seen.

*Will Ford be able to stick it out in the country
to find out more about Autumn?
Find out in HIS HOLIDAY BRIDE
by bestselling author Jillian Hart,
available in October 2010
only from Love Inspired®.*

SHLIEXP1010

# BARBARA
# HANNAY

## *A Miracle for His Secret Son*

Freya and Gus shared a perfect summer, until
Gus left town for a future that couldn't include
Freya.... Now eleven years on, Freya has a life-
changing revelation for Gus: they have a son,
Nick, who needs a new kidney—a gift only his
father can provide. Gus is stunned by the news,
but vows to help Nick. And despite everything,
Gus realizes that he still loves Freya.

**Can they forge a future together and
give Nick another miracle...a family?**

*Available October 2010*

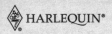